MW00810205

BLACK AMERICA SERIES

PHILADELPHIA

1639–2000

THE PENNSYLVANIA
ABOLITION SOCIETY
&
THE PENNSYLVANIA
BLACK

THE TITLE PAGE FROM THE PENNSYLVANIA ABOLITION SOCIETY'S 200TH ANNIVERSARY EXHIBITION BOOKLET. As the oldest organization of its kind in the United States, the Pennsylvania Abolition Society commemorated its bicentennial in an exhibition held at the Pennsylvania Historical Society in 1974. Members of the society have included such notables as Benjamin Franklin, Thomas Paine, Dr. Benjamin Rush, the Marquis Lafayette, and later, Lucretia Mott.

BLACK AMERICA SERIES

PHILADELPHIA

1639–2000

Charles L. Blockson

ISBN 0-7385-0472-6

First printed in 2000.

Published by Arcadia Publishing,
an imprint of Tempus Publishing, Inc.
2 Cumberland Street
Charleston, SC 29401

Printed in Great Britain.

Library of Congress Catalog Card Number: 00-104075

For all general information contact Arcadia Publishing at:
Telephone 843-853-2070
Fax 843-853-0044
E-Mail sales@arcadiapublishing.com

For customer service and orders:
Toll-Free 1-888-313-2665

Visit us on the internet at http://www.arcadiapublishing.com

A Bust of Bishop Richard Allen. This bust of Bishop Richard Allen is displayed in the museum of the African Methodist Episcopal Church, located at the corner of Sixth and Lombard Streets in Philadelphia.

Contents

Liberation of A Slave

To all people, to whome these presants may come Greeting
know ye That we J. M. of the City of Phia Esqr and C. K. of the
Same place Exr. of the las will and Testament of J. K. Esqr.
Counsellor at Law late of the State of New Jersey deceased—
Sundry good causes and waighty Considerations us hereunto Moving
Have, and by these presants do manumit and from a state of Slavery
liberate and set free Two certain famale Negro slaves the one na-
-med Temp aged about 14 years the other named Susan aged
about 3 years. late the property of the said J. K. Esqr.
Witness our hand & Seals this 13th day of June—
in the year of our Lord 1782—

Sealed & delivered
in the presants of

Power of Attorney at Law

Know all men by these

"Liberation of a Slave." Shown is the work "Liberation of a Slave." (Courtesy of the Historical Society of Pennsylvania.)

One

People of African Descent in Colonial Philadelphia: 1639–1776

Philadelphia has a long and interesting history pertaining to people of African descent, some of whom were slaves of the Swedes, Finns, and Dutch who settled in the city. Africans had been brought to the Delaware River Valley by these Europeans, who had established the first permanent settlements in the area as early as 1639. This was many years before English Quakers, under the leadership of William Penn, were welcomed ashore in 1681. Records of the full names of these colonial enslaved Africans were rarely, if ever, kept. Patrick Robinson, a Swedish slave owner, recorded the name of a slave, Robert Nevergood, in a 1683 census. In 1639, another recorded enslaved "Negro" named "Anthony" had arrived in the New Sweden colony, which was to become Delaware. In 1644, Anthony served Gov. Johan Printz at Tinicum, on the present border with Pennsylvania, making hay for the cattle, and accompanying the governor on his yacht. Other enslaved Africans were soon to follow Anthony, or "Antonio the Moor." They were owned by such notables as the Norris, Inglis, McCall, Turner, Wistar, Van Pelt, Butler, and Meade families.

Three years after the first English Quaker settlers arrived in 1694, 154 enslaved Africans were brought to Philadelphia on the ship *Isabella*. In the years to follow, many prominent Philadelphia merchants and religious and political figures were involved in the trade of African men, women, and children. As were many of the members of his Society of Friends, William Penn was a slave owner in his life, despite his strong religious convictions, but drew up a will granting them freedom upon his death. Robert Morris, in later years known as the "Financier of the Revolution," staked his personal fortune to the cause of the freedom of the slaves, even though part of Morris's wealth had been earned by the firm of Morris and Willing, which imported slaves into Pennsylvania in large numbers between 1754 and 1766.

Stephen Girard, a Frenchman by birth, and although successful in trade in the West Indies, became one of the richest Americans of his time. Girard owned 30 slaves in New Orleans. John Bartam, colonial America's botanical genius, held humans in bondage, as did artist Charles Wilson Peale, one of the most popular and successful painters in colonial America. (Moses Williams, Peale's personal slave, under Peale's guidance, became an expert silhouette maker and was able to purchase his own freedom.) James Logan, William Penn's secretary, built his home Stenton between 1723 and 1730 in Germantown. At Stenton, from whence Gen. William Howe directed the Battle of Germantown, a plaque is dedicated in honor of Logan's slave, Dinah, who saved the mansion from being burned by the British in the winter of 1777.

Even Benjamin Franklin, who drew lightening from the sky and signed the Declaration of Independence, owned slaves early in his life. He was also openly accused of keeping his black maid, Barbara, as a concubine in two pamphlets: *What is Sauce for the Goose, is also Sauce for the Gander* (1764) and *A Humble Attempt at Scurrility* (1765). Shortly before the Revolutionary War, under the influence of two anti-slavery leaders, Anthony Benezet of Philadelphia and Granville Sharp of England, Franklin's attitude toward slavery changed permanently. He was elected to the Pennsylvania Abolition Society in 1787 and later served as the society's president. In 1789, shortly before his death, Franklin sent a petition to Congress that he signed as president of the Pennsylvania Abolition Society. The pamphlet urged Congress to exert the full extent of the power vested in them by the Constitution to discourage the traffic of human beings as slaves.

In colonial Philadelphia during American Revolution, African Americans were often viewed as subhuman, as mankind's lowest "species." At Second and High Streets (now Market Street) stood "the whipping post." The Court of Quaker Sessions on July 4, 1693, stated, "The Constable of Philadelphia or any other person whatsoever is given power to take up Negroes, male or female, whom they should gather about the first days of the week, without a pass from their Mr. or Mrs. [Master or Mistress], or not in their company, or are to carry them to the gallows, there remain that night, and that without meat or drink and to cause them to be publicly whipped the next morning with 39 lashes well laid on their backs."

Formerly located at South Front Street, the London Coffeehouse was built in 1702 by Charles Reed, who obtained the land from William Penn's daughter, Laetitia. The coffeehouse featured a platform where enslaved Africans were sold. Another slave auction block once stood on Water Street between Spruce and Market Streets. Buyers were permitted to pull limbs and examine their "goods," who were usually completely naked. Buyers also checked in the most intimate places for diseases or disability. The slaves that were not sold immediately were put into compounds until a buyer could be found. These compounds were fenced off rectangles and were located not far from the auction area, where now the Liberty Bell rests—the historic symbol that America so reverently preserves as a symbol of human rights and human freedom.

In fact, the Liberty Bell was commissioned by a slaveholder, Isaac Norris, when he was the speaker of the Pennsylvania Assembly. First hung in 1753, this bell bore the inscription,

"Proclaim Liberty throughout the land unto all that inhabitant thereof!" Exactly how this bell got its name is unknown; however, the earliest reference to the Liberty Bell is with a radical anti-slavery group known as the Friends of Freedom, who called for immediate liberation of the slaves. Founded in Boston in 1839, this group of literacy writers and abolitionists issued a series of publications entitled *Liberty* and *Friends of Freedom*. Included in the 1839 issue of the annual publication was a sonnet that was "Suggested by the inscription on the Philadelphia Liberty Bell."

Located near the Liberty Bell and Independence Hall is Washington Square, originally called Congo Square, where during the colonial period, enslaved Africans prayed and danced. (The name Congo referred to that part of Africa now called Zaire.) Free African food vendors cooked traditional African foods and conversed in various languages with their enslaved kinsfolk. African American vendors have a distinguished tradition in Philadelphia at Congo Square and other locations. Another gathering place for these early vendors was the open market place at Head House Square. Here, among other venders, the "pepper-pot women," selling pepper-pot soup, could be found.

Most of the enslaved Africans in Philadelphia and elsewhere in Pennsylvania did not come directly from Africa, but rather from the British West Indies. There they underwent a "seasoning," or what some historians call a "conditioning process." Then, the slaves entered through the Port of Philadelphia in the area now called Penn's Landing. One early slave, "Alice of Dunk's Ferry," as she was called, became one of the elders of Philadelphia's African American community. This remarkable woman was born a slave in 1688 of parents who had been brought from Barbados. She died at the age of 116 in Bristol, Bucks County, in 1804. She lived in Philadelphia until the age of ten, when her owner moved her to Dunk's Ferry, 17 miles up the Delaware River in Bucks County. She spent most of her adult life collecting tolls at the Dunk's Ferry Bridge with the affectionate title Alice of Dunk's Ferry. Alice could be seen riding every Sunday morning on horseback to attend her beloved Christ Church in Philadelphia, when it was still a wooden structure. She enjoyed sharing her vivid memories of William Penn and the early days of the colony, and many were touched by her stories and wisdom.

Some whites thought that the horror of human slavery was a shameful outrage, and they did something about it. In 1688, the "Germantown Protest" was just the first of a number of voices raised in Pennsylvania, to be followed by the writings of John Woolman, Anthony Benezet, George Keith, Benjamin Lay, George Sandiford, Thomas Paine, and others. The Declaration of Independence had noble words on equality of all men, but neither it nor the American Revolution was designed to bring freedom to African Americans in Philadelphia or elsewhere in the colony.

At the beginning of the Revolution, men who were sick and tired of witnessing slavery formed an organization called the "Pennsylvania Society for Promoting the Abolition of Slavery; the Relief of Negroes Unlawfully Held in Bondage; and for Improving the African Race." In 1775, the organization became known as the Pennsylvania Abolition Society. Five years later, the Pennsylvania legislature passed a bill calling for gradual abolition, an omen of full promise. On that occasion, two prominent Pennsylvanians were active on the legislature, Benjamin Franklin and Thomas Paine. Both were appointed to the Abolition Society in 1787. Dr. Benjamin Rush was one of one of the secretaries of the society. The Free

African Community of Philadelphia admired him for his dedication to the cause of freedom.

Progress toward full abolition was slow, since enslaved African Americans were easy to handle politically, for they had neither the vote nor any hope of it. Freed African Americans were much harder to handle, for they had all the qualifications for the vote as their white neighbors, except for white skin. Nevertheless, African Americans remained loyal to their adopted country. Under leadership of respected African Americans in the community, former slaves and freed men such as Rev. Richard Allen, Rev. Absalom Jones, James Forten, Cyrus Bustill, William Gray, and others participated in the bloody quest for freedom for their country, even though that freedom would not come for nearly a century.

ALICE OF DUNK'S FERRY. Alice, as she was called, lived so long that she became an oral historian and a curiosity of her day. She was born in Philadelphia in 1688 of slave parents who had been brought from Barbados. She lived in Philadelphia until age ten, when her master moved her to Dunk's Ferry. When she grew older, she collected tolls at the Dunk's Ferry Bridge. Alice vividly recalled the founder of the state, William Penn. She is remembered to have ridden to her beloved Christ Church on Sunday mornings, even at the age of 95. She could give the details of the wooden structure of the church to anyone who would listen. Alice died at age 116 in 1804.

The Slave Auction. John Rogers, a white sculptor from New England, expressed his anti-slavery sentiment in his work *The Slave Auction,* one of a series of sculptures dealing with the controversy. The sculpture was offered for sale two weeks after John Brown's execution. John Brown had many African-American friends in Philadelphia. Brown's last visit to the city was a year before he was captured and hanged at Harper's Ferry, Virginia, in 1859 for his ill-fated attempt to secure weapons from the Federal arsenal to liberate the slaves. (Courtesy of the William Penn Museum.)

Two

The Era of the American Revolution: 1776–1800

In 1780, Philadelphia's African American population of about 3,000 was concentrated in the area between Fifth and Ninth Streets, from Pine to Lombard Streets. The population doubled in the next ten years, spreading west across Broad Street to form a center of African American business activity at Sixteenth and Seventeenth Streets and a residential district in the southwestern section of the city. By 1793, the spread took a northward trend, when one-quarter the African American population was living between Market and Vine Streets.

The growing African American community, though degraded and subjugated, became quite valuable to whites during this time, and they proudly served their adopted country. The part African Americans played in defense of the United States goes back to the American Revolution. Over 5,000 African Americans throughout the colonies fought in the Revolution. They were fighting side by side with their white comrades in most units of the Continental Army. By the summer of 1778, hardly a ship sailed in the Continental Navy without an African American gunner, officer's helper, or seaman. Among the brave was James Forten. Forten served as a powder boy under Stephen Decatur, commander of the *Pennsylvania Royal Louis*. As an adult, Forten became Philadelphia's most influential African American citizen. Born in Philadelphia in 1762, James Derham, as a child, was sold away from his family to Dr. John Kearsley, who trained him to be his assistant. At the time of the Revolution, Dr. Kearsley enlisted with the British and took Derham with him. After the British were defeated, Derham was sold again to another physician who also taught Derham medical skills. After attaining his freedom, he developed a large and successful practice specializing in tropical diseases. Cyrus Bustill hauled wagonloads of bread from his Arch Street bakery to George Washington's army in Valley Forge. Richard Allen hauled salt from Rehoboth, Delaware, to Valley Forge. While Samuel Fraunces operated his famous tavern in New York City, he entertained George Washington, General Lafayette, and other prominent military officers before moving to Philadelphia after the war. In 1783, many enslaved and freed Africans who remained loyal to the British left Philadelphia along with hundreds of others on ships bound for Nova Scotia. One scholar revealed that 27 African Americans from Philadelphia left, joining 14,000 others of African descent.

Seventeen eighty-seven was an important, but dehumanizing year for African Americans in Philadelphia and other areas of the Commonwealth of Pennsylvania. When the first Continental Congress met in Philadelphia in the summer that year, the northern delegates contended that slaves were property and therefore should not be counted in apportioning representation. A compromise, the first of many that slavery was to bring about, was reached: "Representatives and direct taxes shall be apportioned among the several states . . . according to their respective numbers which shall be determined by adding the whole number of free persons . . . three-fifths of all other persons." These "other persons" were slaves. The slave trade was then extended for 20 years.

In response to disgraces and setbacks like this "compromise," and the segregated worship policy adopted by St. George's Methodist Episcopal Church, Richard Allen and Absalom Jones, along with James Forten, participated in the organization of the African Lodge of Prince Hall Masons and the Free African Society. Proclaiming the uplift of people of African descent, their response was one of the earliest examples of Black Nationalism in America. Free African Society activities included mutual aid. For example, members assisted in the yellow fever epidemic of 1793. They were proud of their African heritage and named their churches, schools, institutions, and societies in honor of the mother continent, Africa.

The horrible yellow fever epidemic of 1793 has been called the worst American epidemic ever. It doomed the supremacy of Philadelphia among American cities. The epidemic began in 1791, as the mulatto and black inhabitants of Hispanola, consisting of St. Domingo (the Spanish part of the island) and St. Dominique (Haiti) started a revolt. The equality promised by the French Revolution encouraged the mulattos and free blacks of the island to seek it for themselves. The decree granting civil rights for mulattos and people of African descent had been so vigorously opposed by the white aristocracy that it had been revoked. In August 1791, a slave rebellion broke out in answer to the revocation. During the revolt, the most hideous atrocities were perpetrated on each other. The English and the Spanish fought against the French, and blacks fought French merchants and plantation owners. The northern provinces' sugar refineries and plantations were destroyed. Cap Francis, the capital of St. Dominique, was rendered to ashes. It was a year of unrelieved chaos. Out of the conflict a great leader emerged, Toussaint L'Ouverture, a former slave. He was named commander-in-chief of the armies, with the assistance of former slaves Jean Jacques Dessaline and Henri Christophe.

French-speaking whites of the island were terrified by the prospect of a Black-led revolution and possible black rule on the island. Vessels carried hundreds of white refugees (or émigrés) their slaves, and even free people of color from Saint Dominique to Philadelphia, New York, Baltimore, Norfolk, and New Orleans. About 600 refugees had entered the city in 1792, in spite of Philadelphia's harsh winter weather and the determination of the city's anti-slavery leaders determined to enforce the Pennsylvania's gradual abolition law of 1780, which guaranteed freedom after six months to any slave owner establishing residence. One historian estimates that at least 848 refugees were of African extraction settled in Philadelphia during this time. Among this group was a number of former slaves and mulattos, for the most part highly literate and more than reasonably prosperous. This became known in Philadelphia as *gen de coleur*.

Stephen Girard, who was born in France, lived on an island off St. Dominique and settled in Philadelphia long before the émigrés of 1793 arrived. He owned slaves at his property in New Orleans. His brother, James, owned slaves who worked on his coffee and sugar plantation in St. Dominique. Stephen Girard employed his brother's black mistress, Hannah, as his personal housekeeper in his large home in Philadelphia. In addition to money willed for Girard College, he bequeathed $200 a year for Hannah until her death.

Most of these French-speaking families settled in the Society Hill section between Second, Fourth, and Race Streets. At first, language was a barrier. A few years earlier, many of the younger refugees had arrived as slaves from Africa to St. Dominique before arriving in Philadelphia with their owners, who had them set free in Philadelphia after six months of residency in compliance with the abolition law. Many brought whatever they could salvage. Some came with skills and trades. Most of these *gen de colour* families attended St. Mary's, St. Peter's, or Holy Cross Catholic Churches, all located within walking distance in their expanding French-speaking communities. Those who brought with them a certain amount of wealth and ambition applied their skills as hairdressers, barbers, and tailors. Women with coffee-colored complexions from Haiti walked around Head House Square with peanut candy cakes in trays balanced on their heads. One account stated that in Philadelphia there were "Mestizo ladies with complexions of palest marble, jet black hair, and eyes of the gazelle, and the exquisite symmetry as well as 'coal black' Negress[es] in flowing white dresses and turbans. Frequently the women were escorted by white, French gentlemen, both dressed richly in West Indian fashion."

Philadelphia's vibrant African, French-speaking community had a profound effect on the freed African American community in the city through religious, political, and cultural means. Peter Albert Augustine acquired wealth and prominence as Philadelphia's leading caterer. Many of the most distinguished foreign guests dined at his establishment, including Napoleon's brother, Joseph, and General Lafayette. Members of another distinguished African American family with French connections were the Dutrieuilles, who were master caterers. (This family later operated the business with the Baptiste family.) Mary A. Dutrieuilles, a schoolteacher during the 1850s, was connected with the anti-slavery movement; she was the only female member of Philadelphia's Vigilance Committee in 1853. Quite a few leading descendants of Philadelphia's French West Indian families—such as the Cuyjets, Montriers, Appos, Dutertes, Baptistes, and the Le Counts—can trace their lineage to residents of Philadelphia.

There were other prominent African Americans in Philadelphia in the early 1800s, such as Robert Bogle, credited with creating the catering profession in America. Ships from Martinique and neighboring islands brought celebrated band leader Frank Johnson and restaurant owner Samuel Fraunces. Edward de Roland, the composer and musician who played in Frank Johnson's band, was a bugler for the mounted troops that paraded through the city's streets. His parents fled from Haiti to Martinique in 1804. In Philadelphia, Edward de Roland was educated at the Willings Alley School, which James Forten also attended.

FIRST PLACE OF MEETING.
FIRST BRICK CHURCH.
Pastors of Bethel Church, Phila., from 1816 to 1899.
RICHARD ALLEN,
RICHARD WILLIAMS,
JACOB TAPSCIO,
WILLIAM CORNISH,
MORRIS BROWN,
JOSEPH COX,
WILLIAM MOORE,
JOHN CORNISH,
WILLIS NAZERY,
HENRY J. YOUNG,
HENRY DAVIS,
RICHARD ROBINSON,
*JOHN CORNISH,
W. D. W. SCHUREMAN,
JOSHUA WOODLAND,
J. P. CAMPBELL,
*WILLIAM MOORE,
* Served two terms.
Pastors of Bethel Church, Phila. from 1816 to 1899.
JAMES HOLLEN,
D. DORRELL,
J. M. WILLIAMS,
*HENRY J. YOUNG,
THEODORE GOULD,
R. F. WAYMAN,
G. C. WHITFIELD,
L. J. COPPIN,
J. S. THOMPSON,
C. C. FELTS,
*J. S. THOMPSON,
J. W. BECKETT,
C. T. SHAFFER,
W. H. HEARD,
W. D. COOK,
*T. GOULD,
*L. J. COPPIN,
* Served two terms.
First Bishop,
Born Feb. 14, 1760. Died Mar. 26, 1831.
Successors :
2. MORRIS BROWN,
3. EDWARD WATERS,
4. WM. PAUL QUINN,
5. WILLIS NAZERY,
6. D. A. PAYNE,
7. A. W. WAYMAN,
8. J. P. CAMPBELL,
9. J. A. SHORTER,
10. T. M. D. WARD,
11. J. M. BROWN,
12. H. M. TURNER,
13. W. F. DICKERSON,
14. R. H. CAIN,
15. R. R. DISNEY,
16. W. J. GAINES,
17. B. W. ARNETT,
18. B. T. TANNER,
19. A. GRANT,
20. B. F. LEE,
21. M. B. SALTER,
22. J. A. HANDY,
23. W. B. DERRICK,
24. J. H. ARMSTRONG,
25. J. C. EMBRY.
BAND TICKET....BETHEL CHURCH.
If ye then be risen with Christ, seek those things which are above, where Christ sitteth on the right hand of God. Col. iii. 1.
Minister.
FAC SIMILE OF FIRST LOVE FEAST TICKET.
THE PRESENT CHURCH.

Richard Allen. Born in 1760 of a "pure African" father and mulatto mother, Allen's family was originally owned by Benjamin Chew, the chief justice of the Pennsylvania Supreme Court. Allen was sold to a man named Stokeley on a plantation in Dover, Delaware. He later bought his freedom and returned to Philadelphia. In 1791, Allen founded the African Methodist Episcopal Church (AME), familiarly known as "Mother Bethel." Allen officially became its minister and promptly bought a site on Sixth Street near Lombard Street. On it was an old frame structure formerly owned by a blacksmith. Allen's congregants restored the building, enlarged it, and opened a house of worship in 1894. Later, Allen became the first bishop of the AME denomination. In 1830, the church was the site of the first black political convention in America, while the building served as a station on the Underground Railroad. The current building was constructed in 1889 in the same location as three previous structures. Mother Bethel sits on the oldest parcel of land in the city continuously owned by African Americans.

SARAH ALLEN. Sarah Allen was born on the Isle of Wight as a slave. No records can be found to ascertain when or how she got her freedom, but she married Allen in 1810 as a free woman. In 1827, she organized the church women, initially to enhance the appearance of the attire of the ministers. Soon, she embraced other mission work, including assisting slaves on the Underground Railroad. The mother of six children, Allen made a mark for herself by playing a significant role in the founding of the Daughters of the Conference organization, part of the AME Church. She died on July 16, 1849.

African American Patriots' Monument. Sponsored the African American women of the Valley Forge chapter of the Delta Sigma Theta sorority, and others, a monument standing 9 feet 6 inches tall and 6 feet wide was erected in Valley Forge National Park. The monument was erected in June 1993 to pay tribute to African American soldiers who "served, suffered and sacrificed," during the Valley Forge encampment of 1777–1778. As many as 800 to 1,000 African American troops endured the bitter winter weather. The monument was designed by artist Cal Massey and completed by sculptor Phillip Sumpter. Both men are well known African American artists in Philadelphia and elsewhere.

Harriet Beecher Stowe, in an introduction to *Colored Patriots of the Revolution* by William C. Nell (1855) wrote, "It was not for their own land they fought, not even for a land which had adopted them, but for a land which had enslaved them and whose laws, even in freedom, oftener oppressed than protected. Bravery under such circumstances has a peculiar beauty and merit."

"Patriots of African Descent." This marker, dedicated by the African American women of the Valley Forge chapter of the Delta Sigma Theta sorority, honors black soldiers who served during the Valley Forge encampment.

Yarrow Mamout. Kidnapped in Africa and sold as a slave in Maryland, Yarrow Mamout kept his Muslim name. He served with the Continental Army as a spy, among other capacities. He became well known through the attention of the Philadelphia artist Charles Peale, who said that he was "interested in Mamout's face because he was a specimen of healthy, cheerful, old age." But something more is caught forever in this portrait. The face of the venerable Moor is shrewd, sad, witty, and a legion of experience. Peale's painting of Mamout is owned by the Historical Society of Pennsylvania at 1300 Locust Street in Philadelphia.

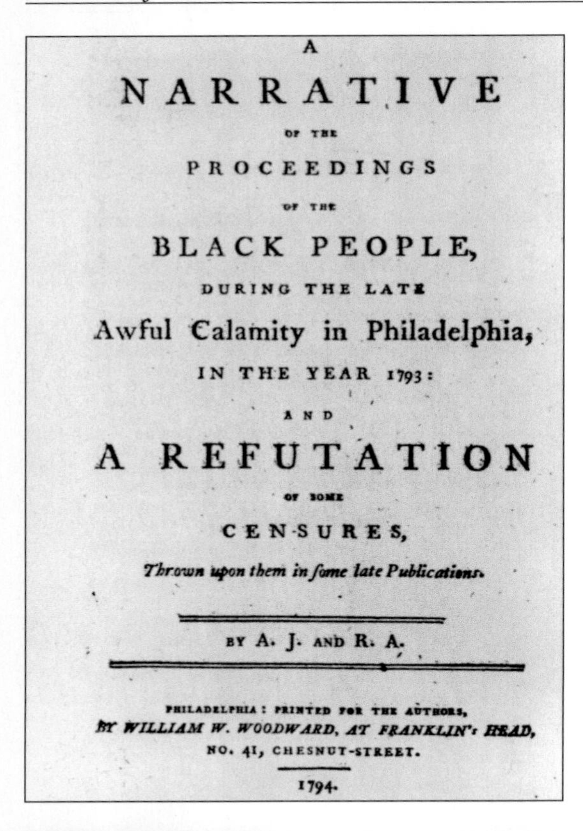
A
NARRATIVE
OF THE
PROCEEDINGS
OF THE
BLACK PEOPLE,
DURING THE LATE
Awful Calamity in Philadelphia,
IN THE YEAR 1793:
AND
A REFUTATION
OF SOME
CENSURES,
Thrown upon them in some late Publications.

BY A. J. AND R. A.

PHILADELPHIA: PRINTED FOR THE AUTHORS,
BY WILLIAM W. WOODWARD, AT FRANKLIN'S HEAD,
NO. 41, CHESNUT-STREET.
1794.

YELLOW FEVER. The yellow fever plague of 1793 was the most appalling collective disaster that had ever overtaken an American city. During the late summer and fall, commerce and government practically ceased. Half of the city's population fled, and 5,000 died. Cries of "bring out your dead" could be heard throughout the city. Led by Richard Allen, Cyrus Bustill, and Absalom Jones, the African American community accepted the challenge of burying the dead—a necessary task far too intimidating for most. They were the first to show courage and leadership to a white community that despised them. After the plague subsided, some whites accused African Americans of stealing money from the plague victims they buried. Allen and Jones jointly wrote *A Narrative of the Proceedings of Black People, During the Late, Awful Calamity in Philadelphia* (1794) in order to refute the slanderous misrepresentation of African Americans' actions during the city's disaster.

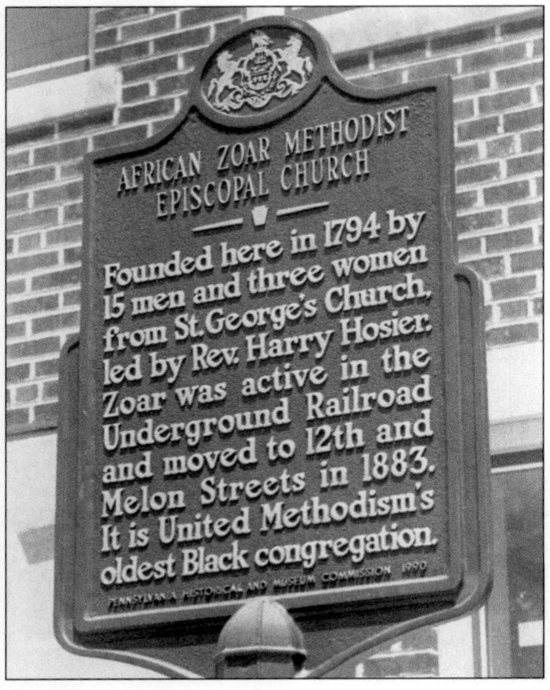

PENNSYLVANIA STATE HISTORICAL MARKER. This state historical marker is for the African Zoar Methodist Episcopal Church. The church was established in 1794, the same time Absalom Jones founded the St. Thomas Church.

ABSALOM JONES. Born a slave in Sussex County, Delaware, on November 6, 1746, Absalom Jones learned to read as a child. At age 16, he was taken to Philadelphia to work in his owner's shop, where a clerk taught him how to write. In 1766, he was allowed to attend night school. His savings enabled him first to purchase his wife's freedom, then his own. In 1792, he founded St. Thomas African Episcopal Church. Jones was ordained the first African American priest of the Episcopal Church in the United States. He also helped to organize the Free African Society with his friend Richard Allen in 1787. Jones was installed as the worship master of the Prince Hall Masonic Lodge. The Reverend Absalom Jones passed away in 1818.

JARENA LEE. Inspired to preach the gospel during her early years, Jarena Lee worked to earn her livelihood as a maid and interim preacher. She was born in Cape May, New Jersey, in 1783. Upon arriving in Philadelphia, she was encouraged to exercise her talent for speaking by Bishop Richard Allen, who was an "early advocate" of equal rights for women. He gave Lee an opportunity to preach at his church. While traveling throughout the eastern seaboard, Jarena preached 178 sermons in one year. She covered 2,325 miles under adverse conditions to deliver her words of wisdom and inspiration.

JAMES FORTEN. During his lifetime, James Forten was one of Philadelphia's most influential African American residents. Born free in 1766, he served as a powder boy under Stephen Decatur during the American Revolution. After leaving the navy, Forten established a very successful business manufacturing sails. It is estimated that his wealth exceeded $100,000, an enormous sum at that time. He employed 40 black and white craftsmen in his business at 95 Wharf Street. During the War of 1812, when British forces threatened Philadelphia, Forten, Richard Allen, and Absalom Jones erected defenses at Gray's Ferry on the Schuylkill River. The Forten home was a mecca for abolitionists, including poet John Greenleaf Whittier, Wendell Phillips, and William Lloyd Garrison. Forten provided funds to support Garrison's anti-slavery newspaper, the *Liberator*.

JAMES FORTEN
(1766 - 1842)
A wealthy sailmaker who employed multi-racial craftsmen, Forten was a leader of the African-American community in Philadelphia and a champion of reform causes. The American Antislavery Society was organized in his house here in 1833.
PENNSYLVANIA HISTORICAL AND MUSEUM COMMISSION 1990

STATE MARKER. This state historical marker honors the site of James Forten's former home.

PAUL CUFFEE. Shown is a silhouette of Paul Cuffee and an image of his ship, the *Traveler*. Cuffee, an African American sea captain of Massachusetts, took 38 black Americans to Sierra Leone, Africa, in 1812. He paid all their expenses in order that they would have a better life. He included among his Philadelphia friends James Forten, Cyrus Bustill, and Rev. Richard Allen.

PRINCE SAUNDERS. Of the various personalities who achieved prominence in Philadelphia, Prince Saunders is one of the least known by today's scholars. Although born of free African American parents in Vermont, Saunders became one of the most renowned educators, lecturers, and politicians of his day. He became a confidant of the eminent black king Henri Christophe of Haiti. Saunders taught Christophe's children and introduced them to vaccination. In 1816, he published the *Haitian Papers*. Two years later, he came to Philadelphia and officiated as a lay reader at St. Thomas Episcopal Church. He published an address delivered at Bethel Church before the Pennsylvania Augustine Society for the Education of People of Color, which he delivered on September 3, 1818. Saunders became one of the first African American schoolteachers in Philadelphia.

PEPPER-POT WOMEN. Among the most interesting street vendors were the pepper-pot women of Head House Square. (A re-creation of that market area is located at Second and Pine Streets.) As they sold their soup, their cries could be heard above all other vendors:

Pepper-pot, all hot, all hot,
makee back strong,
makee live long,
Come buy my Pepper-pot.

Samuel Fraunces. In Gen. George Washington's life, next to his faithful slave William Lee, there was Samuel Fraunces. He was born in the Caribbean of black and white parents and was affectionately known as "Black Sam." Keeping with the fashion of the time, he wore a powdered wig. Fraunces owned one of the finest taverns in colonial New York City. When Washington arrived in Philadelphia in 1790 as president, Fraunces came with him as his personal cook, and established a business referred to as "Tavernkeeper, 166 South," then moved the next year to 59 South Water Street in New York. He named it the Golden Tun Tavern. Fraunces died a few months after the tavern opened.

Robert Bogle. The catering business has been intimately linked with the history of Philadelphia from the earliest times until today. African Americans were the largest component of the catering business in its early years. The American style of "good eating" was exemplified at the table of Robert Bogle's establishment. In 1813, near the northwest corner of Eighth and Sansom Streets, one could find Bogle's restaurant. Stately and polished in manner, Bogle was the leading caterer of his day. A fair-skinned man, Bogle was especially skilled at making meat pies, but he is best known as being a master of ceremonies at weddings and funerals. His clients were usually quite wealthy. Nicholas Biddle, a wealthy banker and poet, wrote a verse in honor of Bogle called "An Ode to Bogle" in 1829.

Above: **The Oyster House.** Other specialties of African American vendors and caterers were fresh clams and oysters. In this lithograph by James Akin from the *Philadelphia Taste Displayer*, or *Bon Ton Below Stairs*, published *c.* 1825, white citizens enjoy samples of oysters as the proud black chef looks on in delight.

Opposite: **Peter Albert Dutrieulle.** Peter Albert Dutrieulle, a descendent of a Haitian family that migrated to Philadelphia in 1793, established a catering business with another Haitian refugee, Peter Augustin, both of whom had made it "in" to be served by "caterers of color." He was an expert carpenter who made coffins and cabinets. The best families of Philadelphia and most distinguished foreign guests, including the Marquis Lafayette, dined at Augustin's establishment. After his death, the Dutrieulle and Baptiste families expanded the business. Descendants of these black refugee families reside in the city today along with the Appos, the Cuyjets, Montiers, Dutertes and Le Counts. These families are called "Old Philadelphians."

THE DUTRIEULLE FAMILY. Dutrieulle family members are pictured standing in front of their catering establishment *c.* 1914. (Albert Dutrieulle Catering Collection, Balch Institute for Ethnic Studies Library.)

DUTRIEULLE SOCIAL CLUB. This turn-of-the-century photograph shows a solemn-looking group of Peter Albert Dutrieulle's Social Club friends. Dutrieulle is shown (first row, second from left) with Andrew Stevens (first row, third from left), Stevens was the president of the Pioneer Building and Loan Association and was also a caterer. (Albert Dutrieulle Catering Collection, Balch Institute for Ethnic Studies Library.)

An African American Woman Entrepreneur. When the Walnut Street Theater opened in 1808, Rachel Lloyd started a restaurant in the theater and continued there until she retired in 1850.

THE
HOUSE SERVANT'S DIRECTORY,
OR
A MONITOR FOR PRIVATE FAMILIES:
COMPRISING
HINTS ON THE ARRANGEMENT AND PERFORMANCE OF
SERVANTS' WORK,
WITH GENERAL RULES FOR
SETTING OUT TABLES AND SIDEBOARDS
IN FIRST ORDER;
THE ART OF WAITING
IN ALL ITS BRANCHES; AND LIKEWISE HOW TO CONDUCT
LARGE AND SMALL PARTIES
WITH ORDER;
WITH GENERAL DIRECTIONS FOR PLACING ON TABLE
ALL KINDS OF JOINTS, FISH, FOWL, &c.
WITH
FULL INSTRUCTIONS FOR CLEANING
PLATE, BRASS, STEEL, GLASS, MAHOGANY;
AND LIKEWISE
ALL KINDS OF PATENT AND COMMON LAMPS:
OBSERVATIONS
ON SERVANTS' BEHAVIOUR TO THEIR EMPLOYERS;
AND UPWARDS OF
100 VARIOUS AND USEFUL RECEIPTS,
CHIEFLY COMPILED
FOR THE USE OF HOUSE SERVANTS;
AND IDENTICALLY MADE
TO SUIT THE MANNERS AND CUSTOMS OF FAMILIES
IN THE UNITED STATES.

BY ROBERT ROBERTS.

WITH
FRIENDLY ADVICE TO COOKS
AND HEADS OF FAMILIES,
AND COMPLETE DIRECTIONS HOW TO BURN
LEHIGH COAL.

BOSTON,

ROBERT ROBERTS: *THE HOUSE SERVANT'S DIRECTORY . . . COMPRISING HINTS ON THE ARRANGEMENT AND PERFORMANCE OF SERVANT'S WORK . . . FRIENDLY ADVICE TO COOKS AND HEAD OF FAMILIES.* Robert Roberts published this book, with its long title, in Boston in 1827. It was the first cookbook by an African American. Roberts's book was widely consulted by caterers in Philadelphia and by wealthy white elite families. Bogle is credited with creating the catering industry in America.

Three

A New Century: Protest, Self-Respect, and Progress: 1800–1865

Philadelphia is often referred to as the cradle of democracy in the United States. Independence Square (now called Independence Mall) is the most historic square mile in the United States and is part of a national historical park. For ten years, from 1790 to 1800, the city served as the nation's capital. However, between 1800 and 1820, after the yellow fever epidemic and partly due to the War of 1812, part of the city's glory had passed. Philadelphia was no longer the capital of the United States. Nevertheless, Philadelphia continued its glory as the largest, wealthiest, and most culturally advanced city in the country. Although the Napoleonic wars in Europe had limited immigration to America, Philadelphia County's population, which includes parts of the present-day bordering counties Montgomery and Delaware, grew from 81,000 in 1800 to 135,637 in 1820. Between 1790 and 1800, the African American population in the Commonwealth of Pennsylvania swelled from 10,000 to more than 16,000 people, most of whom were free. Before the Gradual Act of 1780, there had been 6,000 in the state. By 1800, their numbers had decreased to 1,700. Although this number would fluctuate dramatically, the African American population of Philadelphia, however larger or small, was about to experience a tumultuous century.

The 19th century began with conflict in the City of Brotherly Love. When the War of 1812 broke out, leading citizens of Philadelphia were asked to help defend the city. Among these were Bishop Richard Allen and the Reverend Absalom Jones. They recruited more than 2,000 African American for the war effort. A number served in the navy on the Great Lakes at the Battle of Lake Erie.

Many African Americans in Philadelphia and elsewhere began to believe that their future lie in emigration, however they were hesitant about returning to their mother countries in Africa. They began to consider Haiti, the new black republic, that had been liberated from French rule through violent and bloody warfare under L'Ouverture Dessaline and Christophe, who had crowned himself king of the island republic in 1810. Prince Saunders, a New England–born African American teacher, became King Christophe's confident and wrote the *Haitian Papers*. In 1818, Saunders came to Philadelphia, taught school, and became a Philadelphia anti-slavery leader. He encouraged emigration to Haiti. (Later, in 1824, he organized "the Emigration to Haiti of the Free People of Colour in the United States.")

Shortly after the War of 1812, an African American sea captain, Paul Cuffee of Massachusetts, had taken 38 African Americans aboard one of his own vessels and set sail for Sierra Leone in Africa. He personally paid all expenses, hoping to help them find a better life. Cuffee made several trips to Africa on his famous vessel, the *Traveler*. The main purpose of Cuffee's experiment in Africa was to remove members of his race from a heavy immigration of Europeans to Philadelphia and other northern cities who competed for employment with black labor and made free African Americans unwelcome. Although Cuffee was a good friend of James Forten and Cyrus Bustill, their beliefs would soon be in great contradiction.

In 1816, the American Colonization Society was organized in Washington, D.C. Its purpose was to find a universally satisfactory solution the problems blacks faced as enslaved or free people. One proposed solution, like that of Cuffee, was to force emigration to Africa. The free African Americans throughout the country strongly opposed the plan; they immediately recognized it as a scheme to get rid of free African Americans and to make the institution of slavery more secure. The American Colonization Society members—and many other European groups—organized a response that espoused the idea that African Americans could not assimilate with whites and that they had no future in this country except as slaves.

A meeting of free men was held on January 17, 1817, at Bethel Church, where James Forten presided. Forten and Richard Allen spoke before an audience of 3,000 Philadelphians. James Forten had declared forcefully in his speech, "Here we were born here and we intend to die here. We would never separate ourselves voluntarily from the slave population of this country; they are our brethren by the ties of consanguinity." With this, the African American response to the plans of the American Colonization Society and men like Cuffee was proclaimed: African Americans were now settled and making lives for themselves, many as free men and women, in their new homeland.

With the growing determination of blacks to remain in the United States, and with the death of their mentor and friend Rev. Absalom Jones on February 13, 1818, James Forten, along with Richard Allen and Russell Parrott, became three of the most active spokespersons of their era encouraging education among the masses. The first public school for African Americans was established on Mary Street in 1822. A second school was opened on Gaskill Street in 1825.

However, the outlook for African Americans remained bleak. Blacks were frequently kidnapped by hired slave stealers, some of whom were African American decoys. The *Philadelphia Gazette* reported numerous kidnappings in the city. Philadelphia mayor Joseph Watson received a letter dated February 15, 1826, informing him that a slave kidnapping ring was operating in Philadelphia, led by Patty Cannon, a woman whose headquarters was located in Delaware. The African American community welcomed the opportunity to alert residents of the city to be aware of these kidnappers through newspapers such as the *Freedom Journal*, founded in 1827, and the *Colored American*, which was followed by William Whipper's *National Reformer*.

During the 1830s and beyond, there were more than a dozen African American churches in Philadelphia, and the African American citizens of the city represented 15,000 of the 38,000 African Americans in Pennsylvania. In the autumn of 1830 at Bethel AME Church, under the leadership of Richard Allen, delegates from seven states met to discuss their problems and to publish "An Address to Free People of Color of These United States." Out of the meeting grew the first convention of color, which convened for six days. The following year, 1831, another convention was held at the church. Unfortunately, Bishop Richard Allen died in June of that year; his leadership was taken over by Hezekiah Grice of Baltimore and Abraham Shadd of Delaware. This second meeting was held during and in response to a string of atrocities. A Southhampton, Virginia slave, Nat Turner, and his followers killed at least 57 white people in 1831. News of the revolt sent Virginia and other slave-holding states into a state of panic. While Nat Turner and his followers were arrested and executed, scores of innocent African Americans were slaughtered in a retaliatory revolt by slave owners. Northern white abolitionist and northern free African American leaders were blamed for exciting Nat Turner to revolt. Therefore, African Americans in Philadelphia were denied the rights to assemble in large groups in 1832, although James Forten had told members of the black community that the right to assemble was still theirs. Then, in August 1832, a riot occurred in an amusement park where a group of whites began a melee. For four days the riot continued, until troops were stationed in various sections of the city.

In 1834, a mob tore down a black meetinghouse near Wharton Street as protest against a growing demand for African American equality. Furthermore, Blacks were also confronted by an increasing number of segregation laws. There was more violence and rebellion on the horizon by 1838. On May 17 that year, a mob of angry abolitionists set fire to Pennsylvania Hall, destroying it. William Lloyd Garrison was among the anti-slavery leaders from all over the country who had come for the dedication of the building. During this year of civil unrest throughout Pennsylvania, the Reform Convention to write a new Pennsylvania constitution inserted the word *white* in the qualifications for the right to vote. Philadelphia African Americans responded under the leadership of Robert Purvis, who issued his now famous "Appeal of Forty Thousand Citizens, Threatened with Disenfranchisement."

When the British Parliament emancipated its slaves in West Indies in 1834, there were celebrations throughout the country within African American communities until the civil war. They abandoned the celebration of the Fourth of July, but chose to celebrate August 1 as a holiday to commemorate West Indian emancipation. One day in the spring of 1839, Cinque—the young, handsome son of a Mendi chief—was captured in Africa and sold into slavery and taken aboard the *Amistad* bound for Cuba. Cinque led a mutiny aboard the ship, wherein all but two of the Spanish crew survived, and ordered his men to steer the ship toward Africa. However, the Spanish sailors steered the ship for 63 days on a zigzagged course to New England. There, the enslaved Africans were captured and charged with mutiny. After a long trial, the Africans were set free. Still, by the fall of 1839, African Americans throughout the North were again showing an interest in emigration, this time to the British

West Indies. But the possibilities of future wealth, freedom, and education in the United States kept most African Americans here to stay. A few men had already achieved considerable individual wealth, such as James Forten, Stephen Smith, William Whipper, Albert Dutrieulle, William Still, John McKee, Rev. Joshua Eddy, Jacob White Sr., James Needham, Robert Bogle, Robert Purvis, and James Prosser. Henrietta Duterte, who became the first African American female undertaker, also acquired a considerable amount of wealth. But these people were unusual, since most free African American men and women existed on meager earnings. Many had attained their freedom with no skills and no education. The churches served as a gathering place to worship, discuss politics, socialize, and organize fraternal organizations, debating clubs, and libraries.

However, during the 1830s, intellectual segments in the community had begun to emerge. For example, the Reading Room Society was organized in 1828. Three years later, the Female Literary Society was founded. Other intellectual and moral societies included the Library Company of Colored Persons (1835), the Demostheian Society (1837), and the Gilbert Lyceum (1841). The Grand United Order of Odd Fellows sprang from the black churches during 1830s. The Institute for Colored Youth was founded in 1837 by concerned whites who appointed Fanny Jackson, (later Coppin) as the institute's principal. She worked with Rev. Matthew Anderson, founder of the Berean Training School (later called the Berean Institute). Men and women of letters published books and pamphlets. Published in 1827 was Robert Roberts's book *The House Servant's Directory,* the first cookbook written by an African American (see page 30). Although Roberts was a native of Massachusetts, the book was widely consulted by Philadelphia's caterers and others. In 1841, Joseph Willson of Baltimore published *Sketches of the Higher Classes of Colored Society in Philadelphia.* In this work, Willson stated, "Taking the body of the colored population in the City of Philadelphia, they present in a gradual, moderate, and limited ration almost every grade of character, wealth and . . . education. They are to be seen in ease, comfort, and enjoyment of all social blessings of this life and in contrast with this, they are to be found in the lowest depths of human degradation, misery and want."

But African Americans who were seen to be emulating the higher classes of Philadelphia's African American elite in other cities were ridiculed by some whites. The lives of African Americans in Philadelphia brought about the creation of separate lifestyles. Even when excluded from the mainstream, they protested for equal treatment. The Quakers insisted that African American members of their society sit on separate meetinghouse benches. Grace Mapps Douglass and her daughter, Sarah Douglass, refused to obey.

Once freed, there was some hope of a better lifestyle, and it was in the working to bring about a movement toward complete and total freedom of enslaved people of color in the South. In the 30 years before the Civil War, black and white abolitionists maintained a fever pitch for their moral outrage over human bondage. Unpopular and controversial and detested by many other Americans, the abolitionists kept to the task. Realizing that neither runaway slaves nor freed African Americans were completely safe in the city, a small group of Quakers worked with the city's African American community and began to organize protection for escaping slaves. An intriguing secret system of the Underground Railroad soon snaked through the city. Because of its location, Philadelphia became one of the most important cities connected to the freedom network. Travel on the Underground Railroad was mostly at night, as runaways had to remain in hiding by day. A number of Philadelphia's African American churches opened their doors to receive the weary travelers from the South. Indeed, the most vociferous organizers of the network to freedom were churchmen. The Philadelphia Vigilance Committee played a vital role in assisting slaves north toward Canada. William Still, the secretary of the committee, kept records of all the "passengers" who came to the Pennsylvania Anti-Slavery Society office located in the city. He later published his massive book *The Underground Railroad* in 1872. There were other prominent African Americans connected to the Underground Railroad: Robert Purvis, president of the Philadelphia Underground Railroad; the legendary Harriet Tubman, who lived in the city from time to time; the Bustill brothers Joseph and Charles; and John P. Burr. Among the African American women connected with the Underground Railroad were Elizabeth Taylor Greenfield, "the Black Swan;" Sarah, Harriet and Margaretta Forten, the daughters of James Forten; Grace and Sara Mapps Douglass; Hester Reckless; Hetty Burr; Lydia White; Henrietta Duterte; and Frances Ellen Harper. These active African Americans were important in the work of J. Miller McKim, Issac Hopper, James and Lucretia Mott, Passmore Williamson, and Anna Dickerson. With the help of unknown members of the Underground Railroad nationwide, an estimated 75,000 to 100,000 slaves escaped to freedom in the decades preceding the Civil War.

Even in wartime, and with help from the African American community desperately needed by whites, segregation and exclusion continued. During the first year of the Civil War, participation by African Americans was limited almost to nonmilitary service. Northerners believed that the conflict would be a "white man's war." In Philadelphia, the Union League championed the cause of African Americans seeking to serve the Union Army. It helped to establish Camp William Penn in Cheltenham Township, Montgomery County, on the land that Lucretia Mott and her family donated to the Federal government. Frederick Douglass came to the city to help raise troops among the black volunteers. Nearly 9,000 black Philadelphians answered his plea. Philadelphia troops saw action for the first time at the bloody battle of Fort Wagner, South Carolina, when they fought as members of the famous 54th Infantry Regiment that was largely composed of African American soldiers who trained at Camp William Penn. David Bustill Bowser, a prominent Philadelphia artist, designed several regimental flags during the war. Christian Fleetwood, a graduate of Lincoln University, was a sergeant major in the Union Army. He was among the first African American winners of the Medal of Honor.

Finally, the Thirteenth Amendment abolished slavery everywhere in the United States. Before his death, Pres. Abraham Lincoln had urged Congress to take such action. As for the slaves themselves, newly free, a new world came into existence. Against southern opposition, the Freedman's Bureau, supported by Federal troops, established schools to educate the newly freed slaves. Charlotte Forten, granddaughter of James Forten, traveled to South Carolina as a teacher. By 1867, almost every county in the South had at least one school for African Americans. Both young and old attended the schools during the Reconstruction era. Freedom and education for all people was far from existent, but there was finally some lasting hope.

Life in Philadelphia. There was a series of dramatic stereotypical broadsides issued in London between 1800 and 1825 depicting African American society in Philadelphia in a highly satirical manner. The broadsides were the forerunners of the mockery of African Americans that became popular minstrel shows, another genre that later appeared in various advertisements. The attractive and colorful clothing featured in this image was worn at the African Fancy Ball, first held in February 1828. One of the dances, "Patting Juba," included the use of hands patting various parts of the body while keeping rhythm with the feet. Only free African Americans who could trace their arrival in America at least one generation were permitted to attend the ball.

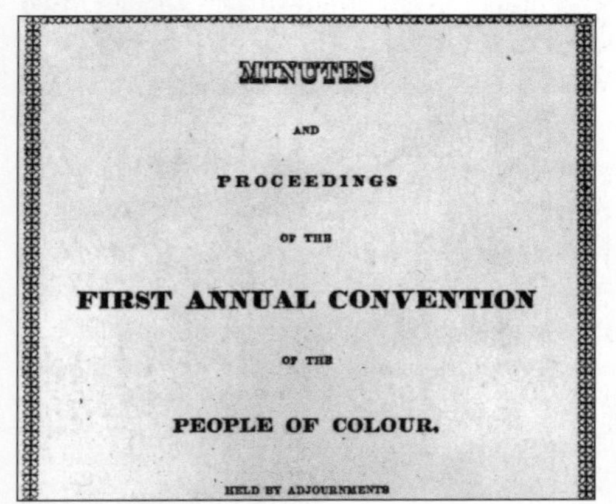

MINUTES

AND

PROCEEDINGS

OF THE

FIRST ANNUAL CONVENTION

OF THE

PEOPLE OF COLOUR,

HELD BY ADJOURNMENTS

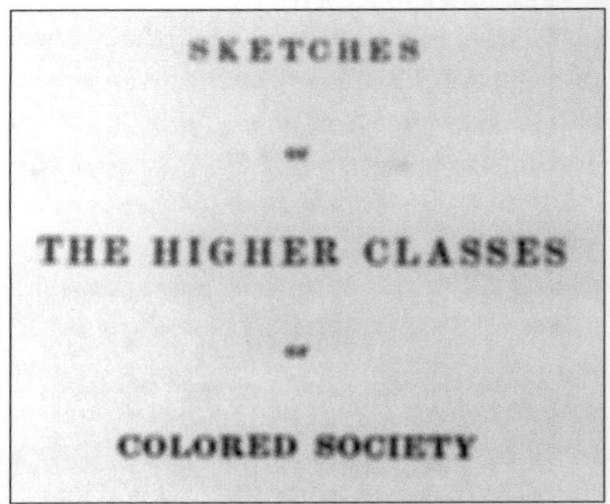

SKETCHES

OF

THE HIGHER CLASSES

OF

COLORED SOCIETY

Left: **First Annual Convention of the People of Colour.** Pictured is a rare pamphlet that illustrates and chronicles the proceedings of the First Annual Convention of the People of Colour. The pamphlet marked a heightening of the intensity of the movement. Cries against kidnapping of free persons and for civil rights were echoed and reechoed throughout the convention. Delegates of the convention vehemently denied any plans for repatriation to Africa. *Right:* ***Sketches Of the Higher Classes of Colored Society in Philadelphia*, by Joseph Willson, an African American, in 1841.** Willson's slender book has been called "one of the best sources of study of inner life of cultured blacks prior to the Civil War." Willson described parties, class attitudes, and cultural institutions of the African American "elite." He wrote his book to combat prejudice from without and to correct abuses within the African American community. Willson arrived in Philadelphia in the late 1830s. At the time his book was published in 1841, Philadelphia's African American population was estimated at 19,000. It was the largest and culturally the most significant of any urban community in the north.

ROBERT PURVIS. Purvis was the son of a free-born woman of African descent and a wealthy Englishman from Charleston, South Carolina. Robert Purvis was very fair-skinned and could have passed as a white man, but he identified with the African American community in Philadelphia. He was brilliant, wealthy, and the son-in-law of James Forten. Purvis was a charter member of the Pennsylvania Anti-Slavery Society, chairman of the Philadelphia Vigilance Committee, and president of the Philadelphia Underground Railroad. He refused to pay taxes when black children were excluded from public schools. In 1834, Robert Purvis and his wife, Harriet, were the first persons of African descent in the United States to receive an official passport. Purvis died at the age of 87 in 1898. He is buried in a Quaker cemetery with his lifetime friend, Quaker Lucretia Mott.

APPEAL

OF

FORTY THOUSAND CITIZENS,

THREATENED WITH

DISFRANCHISEMENT,

TO THE

PEOPLE OF PENNSYLVANIA.

PHILADELPHIA:
PRINTED BY MERRIHEW AND GUNN,
No. 7 Carter's Alley.

1838.

***APPEAL OF FORTY THOUSAND CITIZENS THREATENED WITH DISENFRANCHISEMENT TO THE PEOPLE OF PENNSYLVANIA* (1838).**
At "a very numerous and respectable meeting of colored citizens of Pennsylvania" on March 14, 1838, Robert Purvis's appeal was read. Purvis's well-phrased, well-argued plea against racial limitation was, considering the provocation, moderate in tone: "We appeal to you from the decision of the 'Reform Convention,' which has stripped us of a right peaceably enjoyed during 47 years under the Constitution of this commonwealth." The appeal for the right to vote fell on deaf ears.

A PUBLIC MEETING

WILL BE HELD ON

THURSDAY EVENING, 2D INSTANT,

7; o'clock, in ISRAEL CHURCH, to consider the atrocious decision of the upreme Court in the

DRED SCOTT CASE,

d other outrages to which the colored people are subject under the Constitu-on of the United States.

.L. REMOND,

ROBERT PURVIS,

d others will be speakers on the occasion. Mrs. MOTT, Mr. M'KIM and .S. JONES of Ohio, have also accepted invitations to be present.
All persons are invited to attend. Admittance free.

The Dred Scott Decision. This broadside announced that a meeting was to be held at the Israel church in the Philadelphia's African American neighborhood. In 1856, U.S. Supreme Court justice Roger Taney's infamous decision ruled that Dred Scott, a former Missouri slave who had become a free man by virtue of residence on free soil, had no rights that a white man was bound to respect. Taney further declared that blacks could not rightfully become citizens of the United States, since the words of the Declaration of Independence and the Constitution were never meant to include blacks. In the north and the west, great mass meetings aroused furious protest among blacks and their sympathizers. Robert Purvis and Charles Lenox Remond, a New England African American abolitionist, organized the protest meeting in Philadelphia. An original copy of this broadside is on display in Mother Bethel AME Church.

CINQUE: THE HERO OF THE *AMISTAD*. The Amistad trial has been acclaimed by historians as the most celebrated slave mutiny case of the 19th century. The case, with its international complications, became a national sensation. In 1839, slaves who had been captured in Africa freed themselves under the leadership of the forceful Cinque. They killed all but two of the crew and took over the Spanish ship *Amistad*. The two spared Spaniards craftily steered the ship to New England instead of Africa. Upon landing, charges of piracy and murder were charged against the Africans. Former U.S. president John Quincy Adams represented the Africans, took the case to Supreme Court, and won. The Africans were declared free men. Robert Purvis, a wealthy African American noted for his involvement in the anti-slavery movement, was so impressed with the leadership of Cinque that he commissioned artist Nathaniel Jocelyn to paint a portrait of Cinque, which was hung in Purvis's Philadelphia home. In 1998, Philadelphia-born sculptor and writer Barbara Chase-Riboud—author of the novel *Echo of Lions*, published in 1989 and based on the Amistad case—brought charges of plagiarism against filmmaker Steven Spielberg's company Dream Works, which had produced a feature film of the event that same year.

The Fire at Pennsylvania Hall. Once located at Sixth and Haines Street, Pennsylvania Hall was built in 1838 as a meeting place for anti-slavery societies and other groups. After several days of speeches in a growing climate of hostility, black and white abolitionists were sitting together and walking the streets together. A mob formed around Pennsylvania Hall on the evening of May 17, 1838, and overwhelmed Mayor Swift and the police protecting the building. The mob broke in and set the building on fire. Pennsylvania Hall was just one of the structures burned by the white mob. Other buildings that were burned were the Shelter for Colored Orphans at Thirteenth and Callowhill Streets, and the African American Church at Seventh and Bainbridge Streets.

Institute for Colored Youth. Cheyney University, as it is called today, was established in Philadelphia in 1837 as the Institute for Colored Youth. It was set up exclusively to train African American teachers. In 1902, the school was relocated to Cheyney, a rural area in Chester County, Pennsylvania, and ultimately became a state teacher's college. The school was originally located at 915 Bainbridge Street in Philadelphia.

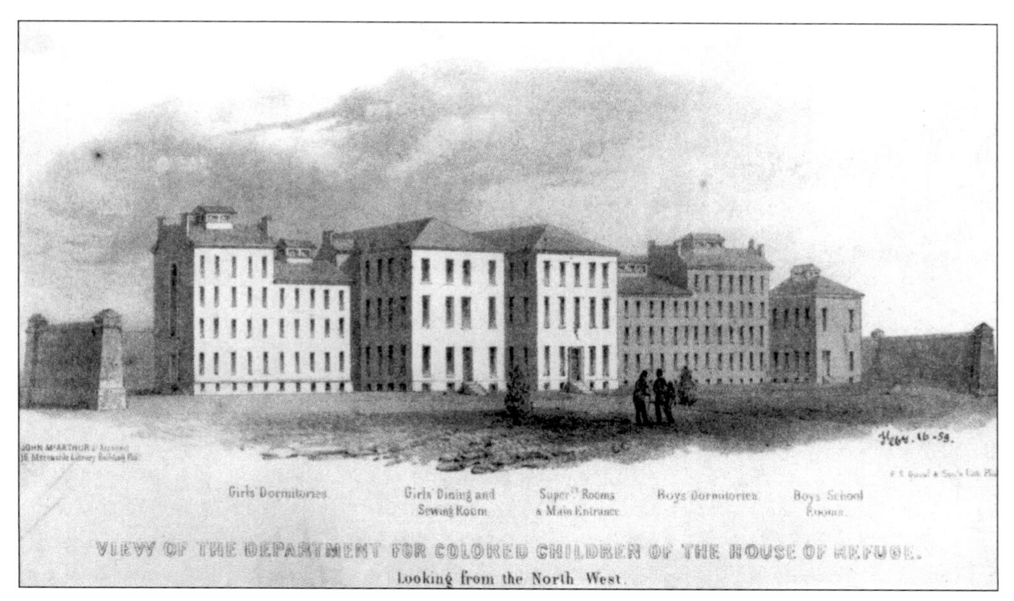

VIEW OF THE DEPARTMENT FOR COLORED CHILDREN OF THE HOUSE OF REFUGE. This scene looks from the northwest and provides an impressive view of the Department for Colored Children of the House of Refuge. Homeless children were admitted to the institution and were taught a variety of trades. This photograph was reproduced in 1859 from a lithograph created by P.S. Duval and Son. Shown is a series of buildings that includes a girls' dormitory, girls' dining room, a sewing room, a supper room, a boys' dormitory, and a boys' school.

Stephen Smith. During his lifetime, Smith was an agent on the Underground Railroad, businessman, philanthropist, and one of the wealthiest African Americans in the United States. He was born in 1797 in Columbia, Lancaster County, Pennsylvania, and went on to build an empire that included the Smith, Whipper & Company lumber and coal yard. In 1867, Smith and his wife, Harriet, donated property and cash totaling $250,000 for the establishment of a home for the aged and infirm. The home, which bears his name, was dedicated two years before his death and still operates today.

WILLIAM WHIPPER. William Whipper was an Underground Railroad agent, moral reformer, and wealthy businessman. He was born in 1804 in Lancaster County, Pennsylvania, and was residing in Philadelphia by 1828. In 1837, he published an article entitled "Non-Resistance to Offensive Aggression" in the *Colored American* newspaper. He viewed the "moral elevation" of his people as a prerequisite to their enjoyment of freedom.

FRANK JOHNSON. Frank Johnson was a major force in early American music. After gaining early experience in a black military band during the War of 1812, Johnson traveled far and wide and built a reputation during the 1800s as a composer, bandleader, fiddler, bugler, and orchestra director. His musical ability so impressed General Lafayette during a performance at Philadelphia Chestnut Street Theater in 1825 that Lafayette sponsored a European tour for him. According to tradition, it was during that tour that Johnson played for Queen Victoria, who presented him with a silver bugle after his performance. When Johnson died, the bugle was buried with him.

TWENTIETH ANNIVERSARY

OF

BRITISH

West India Emancipation!!

The glorious First of August! the day upon which every Bondman in the British Dominion was freed from his chains by Act of Parliament, through the labors of Wilberforce, Clarkson, Brougham and other noble philanthrophists, will be celebrated (in consequence of the first coming on Sunday,)

On MONDAY, AUGUST 2nd, 1858,

BY THE

BANNEKER INSTITUTE,

In the New and Beautiful Grove, known as

HADDINGTON MANSION.

☞This new, romantic and delightful place of resort, is situated in the 24th Ward, at the terminus of the West Philadelphia Passenger Railway. It is in form, nearly circular, and is enclosed by thick woods, and finely cultivated farms. The surrounding country is hilly, beautiful and picturesque in the extreme. A small stream slowly winds its way along the southern edge of the Grove, in which are several miniature cataracts, There is an excellent platform, (which is finely shaded by overhanging trees,) with swings and everything requisite for the pleasure of a Pic-Nic Party. There is also, a large and fine Hotel, with a cupalo commanding a most excellent view of the adjacent country, and in which shelter can be taken in case of a shower All these features, together with its comparative nearness, makes "Haddington Mansion" just the place to spend a day away from the city's heat and din, and constitute it the best resort of the kind in the vicinity of Philadelphia.

The members of the Banneker call upon all the lovers of Freedom and Reform to give support to this movement by honoring them with their presence at the Grove on the day of celebration.

The EXERCISES will commence at 11 o'clock.

The INTRODUCTORY REMARKS will be made by Mr. Wm. H. Minton.

Reading the ACT OF EMANCIPATION, by Mr. Jacob C. White, Jr.

ADDRESSES by Messrs. S. P. Cornish, J. C. Bowers, G. E. Stevens, and S. G. Gould.

The Rev. Wm. Scuman, Rev. Jesse Bolden, and I. C. Wears, Esq., have also been invited to make Addresses.

AN EXCELLENT ORCHESTRA IN ATTENDANCE.

☞Excursionists will take the CARS at EIGHTH and MARKET STREETS.

TICKETS, 37½ CENTS,

To be had at the Lebanon Cemetery Office; at the Segar Store of Mr. Geo. Goines, 6th above Lombard; at the S. W. Cor. of Robison and Poplar Streets, and of the following

The Twentieth Anniversary of British West Indies Emancipation. On August 1, 1833, an act of Parliament abolished slavery in the British West Indies. The anniversary of this event became a more important holiday than the Fourth of July to African Americans since it seemed hypocritical to celebrate Independence Day when slaves were still held in the South. This broadside, issued in 1858, announces a picnic and program of entertainment for the West Indies Emancipation Day sponsored by the Banneker Institute of Philadelphia.

ELIZABETH TAYLOR GREENFIELD. This remarkable woman was born a slave in Natchez, Mississippi, in 1809 and was later adopted by a Quaker woman who brought her to Philadelphia. Greenfield's great singing career began with performances at local gatherings. She was recognized for having an unused voice range of three and one-quarter octaves. Newspaper critics named her the Black Swan, and the affectionate title remained with the singer throughout her life. Taylor appeared before Queen Victoria in England in 1854. In Philadelphia, she was connected with the Underground Railroad and helped raise funds for African American soldiers during the Civil War. This broadside advertised the appearance of the Black Swan, who became a legend during her lifetime.

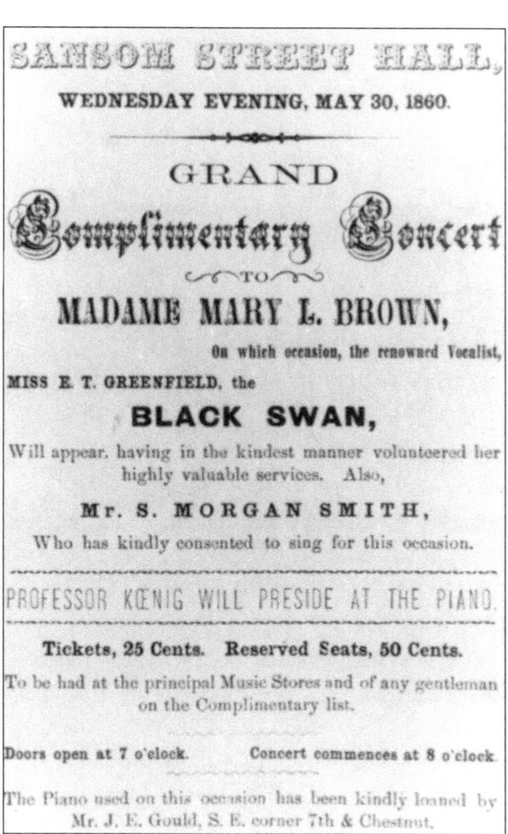

SANSOM STREET HALL,

WEDNESDAY EVENING, MAY 30, 1860.

GRAND

Complimentary Concert

TO

MADAME MARY L. BROWN,

On which occasion, the renowned Vocalist,

MISS E. T. GREENFIELD, the

BLACK SWAN,

Will appear, having in the kindest manner volunteered her highly valuable services. Also,

Mr. S. MORGAN SMITH,

Who has kindly consented to sing for this occasion.

PROFESSOR KŒNIG WILL PRESIDE AT THE PIANO.

Tickets, 25 Cents. Reserved Seats, 50 Cents.

To be had at the principal Music Stores and of any gentleman on the Complimentary list.

Doors open at 7 o'clock. Concert commences at 8 o'clock.

The Piano used on this occasion has been kindly loaned by Mr. J. E. Gould, S. E. corner 7th & Chestnut.

WILLIAM STILL. William Still was born in New Jersey and came to Philadelphia in 1844. He taught himself to read and write, took a job as a clerk for the Pennsylvania Anti-Slavery Society, and soon became one of the most important figures in the Underground Railroad. He kept detailed records of every escaped slave passing through Philadelphia, which is preserved in his classic book *The Underground Railroad*, published in 1872. The book was published after Still had become a prosperous businessman. One of the most dramatic incidents in Still's career with the Underground Railroad was his reunion with his brother, Peter, who had been kidnapped and sold as a slave 40 years earlier.

Librarian of Congress. Copyright Office. United States of America.

Library of Congress,
Washington, April 11th, 1872.

William Still Esq.
Care of Porter & Coates, 822 Chestnut St.
Philadelphia.

The undersigned hereby acknowledges the receipt of two copies of

Underground Railroad

transmitted by you to this Library, in conformity with the laws of the United States respecting Copyrights.

Very respectfully,

A R Spofford

Librarian of Congress.

HARRIET TUBMAN. Harriet Tubman was known as "Moses" to her people. She was born a slave in Maryland and as a young woman fled north to freedom, passing through Philadelphia in 1849. At least 19 times, Tubman returned south to conduct perhaps 300 slaves, including her own family, on the Underground Railroad. On various occasions, she lived and worked for short periods in Philadelphia, attended church, and worked closely with agent William Still and other Underground Railroad leaders.

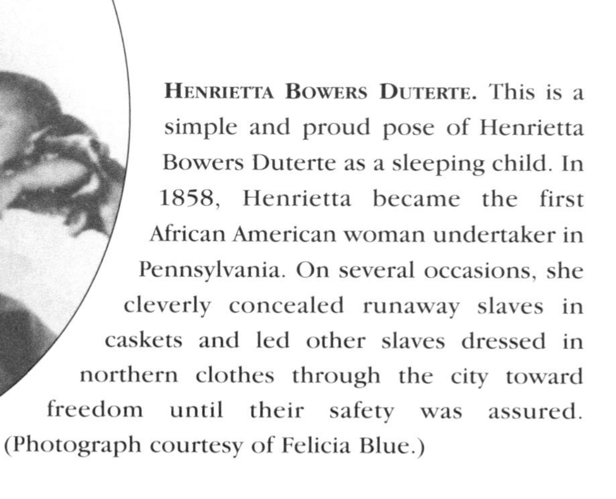

HENRIETTA BOWERS DUTERTE. This is a simple and proud pose of Henrietta Bowers Duterte as a sleeping child. In 1858, Henrietta became the first African American woman undertaker in Pennsylvania. On several occasions, she cleverly concealed runaway slaves in caskets and led other slaves dressed in northern clothes through the city toward freedom until their safety was assured. (Photograph courtesy of Felicia Blue.)

HENRY "BOX" BROWN. One of the most daring and ingenious escapes on the Underground Railroad occurred in 1848, when Henry Brown, a "model slave" from Richmond, Virginia, had himself nailed in a box with a bladder of water and a few biscuits and shipped to the Philadelphia Vigilance committee. Although he traveled upside down part of the way, he arrived safely after a terrifying ride on the railroads. He was rescued by anti-slavery leaders, who christened him Henry "Box" Brown. He was later invited to several African American churches in the city to demonstrate how he made his perilous journey on the Underground Railroad. One of Brown's saviors, William Still (standing in the rear), worked tirelessly with escapees, keeping records to guide their relatives. However, the white Virginian who helped Brown, Samuel A. Smith, was sentenced to prison for a subsequent attempt to freight slaves to freedom.

FRANCES ELLEN WATKINS HARPER. Lecturer, poet, writer, temperance reformer, and teacher Frances Harper was born free in Baltimore, Maryland, and became the first African American woman instructor in vocational education at the African Methodist Episcopal Union Seminary near Columbus, Ohio. This remarkable, self-educated woman was referred to as the "Brown Muse" and described as "a petite, dignified woman whose sharp black eyes and attractive face revealed her sensitive nature." Harper came to Philadelphia, lived in an Underground Railroad station, and ultimately became a conductor. Her friend William Still wrote that she was "one of the most liberal contributors as will as one of the ablest advocates for the Underground Railroad and the slave." Later in her life, Harper was active in the establishment of the National Association of Colored Women and became its vice president. She is remembered for her famous poems "The Slave Mother" and "Bury Me in a Free Land."

FREDRICK DOUGLASS. Fredrick Douglass, an escaped slave from Maryland, became a skilled abolitionist speaker praised for his "wit, argument, sarcasm, and pathos." He urged African Americans to pursue vocational education and the vote. In fact, his print shop in Rochester, New York, was a station on the Underground Railroad. Douglass lived in Philadelphia for a short period in 1863. He told African American ministers and other leaders within the community, "If colored men did not enlist in the Union Army, they would not be able to claim complete freedom after the war had been won." Two of Douglass's sons served with the celebrated 54th Infantry Regiment. Many of the soldiers in the regiment received their training at Camp William Penn.

MEN OF COLOR

IN CONSEQUENCE OF

INDISPOSITION,

OF

FRED'K DOUGLASS

The Meeting for Promoting Recruiting for

3d REGIMENT

U.S. COLORED TROOPS

IS POSTPONED UNTIL

FRIDAY, JULY 24, 1863.

MEN OF COLOR, TO ARMS! NOW OR NEVER! On June 17, 1863, a company of African Americans under the command of Capt. A.M Ball applied for uniforms and arms at the Philadelphia City Arsenal. This was the first local company of African American troops enrolled in the army. Frederick Douglass came to Philadelphia to encourage the enlistment of African Americans in the service of the Union and the cause of emancipation. Those who signed the call to arms were the most distinguished African Americans in Philadelphia. "This is our golden

MEN OF COLOR

OF PHILADELPHIA!

The Country Demands your Services. The Enemy is Approaching. You know his object. It is t
Subjugate the North and Enslave us. Already many of our Class in this State have been Capture
and Carried South to Slavery, Stripes and Mutilation. For our own sake and for the sake of ou
Common Country we are called upon now to

COME FORWARD!

Let us seize this great opportunity of vindicating our manhood and patriotism through all time
The General Commanding at this post is arranging for the

DEFENCE OF THE CITY!

He will need the aid of every Man who can shoulder a musket or handle a pick. We have assure
him of the readiness of our people to do their whole duty in the emergency. We need not ask yo
to justify us in having made this assurance. The undersigned have been designated a Committe
to have this matter in charge. Members of this Committee will sit every day at

BETHEL CHURCH, cor. of 6th & Lombard Streets

AND AT

UNION CHURCH, Coates Street below York Avenue

Their business will be to receive the Names of all Able Bodied Men of Color who are willing to share with others the burdens and duties of Entrenching and Defending the City. Men of Color! you who are able and willing to fight or labor in the work now to be done, call immediately and report yourselves at one or the other of the above named places.

moment," they shouted. "A new era is open to us . . . . Let us rush to arms! Fail now and our race is doomed on this soil of our birth!" Thousands of copies of this broadside entitled "Men of Color" were distributed in the city. The supervisory committee, along with leaders of the African American community, eventually recruited 8,000 Union soldiers. Despite valiant service, African American regiments were not permitted to march in the city's welcome home parade at war's end.

MILITARY SCHOOL FOR OFFICERS OF NEGRO TROOPS. The headquarters for the Supervisory Committee for Recruiting Colored Troops and Free Military School for Applicants for Command of Colored Troops was once located at 1210 Chestnut Street. The members of the Union League were on the recruitment committee. "This is our golden moment," echoed Fredrick Douglass, who came to Philadelphia for the historic recruitment.

CAMP WILLIAM PENN. On June 19, 1863, a meeting was held and a committee of prominent men was appointed to create black regiments. Camp William Penn was located well out of sight of the citizens of Philadelphia in Cheltenham Township in Montgomery County, bordering Philadelphia. No less than 11 regiments were formed at Camp William Penn before the end of the war—the 3rd, 6th, 8th, 22nd, 24th, 25th, 32nd, 41st, and 127th Infantries. Today, several state historical markers and a small museum honor this former campsite where 11,000 black soldiers trained.

DAVID BUSTILL BOWSER. David Bustill Bowser, a member of one of Philadelphia's prominent African American families, was one of the leading artists of his day. As a student, Bowser studied under his cousin, Robert M. Douglass Jr., of Philadelphia. Bowser painted portraits of the famous abolitionist John Brown, who sat for the painting in Bowser's home while visiting anti-slavery friends in Philadelphia. In addition to painting regimental flags for the U.S. Colored Troops during the Civil War, Bowser was a painter of emblems and banners for firemen's companies and fraternal organizations of Philadelphia.

UNITED STATES COLORED TROOPS REGIMENTED FLAG. Painted by artist David Bustill Bowser, this flag represents the colors of the 6th U.S. Colored Troops Infantry Regiment. Bowser was commissioned by the Philadelphia Supervisory Committee for Recruiting Negro Troops to paint various regimented flags. Casualties suffered by the black regiments totaled 2,492. Of that number, 926 died of disease such as scurvy, malignant fever, and dysentery; 440 were missing or captured; and 654 were wounded. Even the regiment's chaplain, Rev. Jerimiah W. Asher, was stricken with malignant fever. Asher was a former pastor of Mother Bethel AME Church.

CHARLOTTE FORTEN. The granddaughter of James Forten, Charlotte was educated at home and in Salem, Massachusetts. She volunteered to go to St. Helena, South Carolina, after the Civil War to teach black children. She returned to Philadelphia in 1864, where she taught school and worked for magazines. She was familiar with famous anti-slavery leaders of her day such as Fredrick Douglass, Lucretia Mott, John Greenleaf Whittier, and others. Her journal, which she began in her school years, became an important historical document. Written between 1854 and 1864, the journal is a unique document from African American woman of that period in history. It reveals how her resentment against the the prejudice of the white world was transformed into a determination to excel.

OCTAVIUS VALENTINE CATTO. Octavius Valentine Catto was one of the first graduates of the Institute for Colored Youth and was later a teacher there. Catto, a political organizer, respected by both the black and white communities, was murdered in a riot during the election of 1871. The marines were called in to prevent further disturbances and the Pennsylvania militia guarded his body. The martyred Catto's funeral was the largest demonstration in Philadelphia since the death of Pres. Abraham Lincoln. Catto held a commission as a major in an all black National Guard unit and was buried with full military honors.

Four

The Quest for Equality: 1865–1900

After the Civil War, prominent politicians and people in power were beginning to question policies of segregation in the newly reunited United States. Pennsylvania congressman William D. Kelley, a native of Philadelphia and one of the founders of the Republican party, supported all measures for the abolition of slavery and equal rights for African Americans. In 1866, Kelley wrote a pamphlet entitled *Why Colored People in Philadelphia Are Excluded from the Street Cars.* Kelley and Rep. Thaddeus Stevens were considered by African Americans to be two of the most sincere white friends that they had in Congress. One white Philadelphia Democrat, Daniel Fox, stated, "If blacks could ride on the cars, there would likely be demands for political equality, including the right to hold office." African American Civil War soldiers were tossed off the trolleys when they attempted to sit down. Fredrick Douglass and African American abolitionist and author William Wells Brown, while visiting the city, were not permitted to ride the trolley cars.

Reaction to this unjust exclusion was growing. Mary Ann Shadd—daughter of the prominent Shadd family of Wilmington, Delaware, and a schoolteacher—once remained in her seat when asked to leave the trolley. William Still and Octavius V. Catto, a Philadelphia schoolteacher and captain of the Pythian Baseball Club, led the public campaign to desegregate the streetcars. In 1871, the city responded violently. Catto, while working for the Republican party, was killed by a man named Frank Kelly during a riot as he walked home. Already a hero within the African American community, Catto became its martyr. His funeral was one of the largest ever held in Philadelphia. Still, only whites were allowed on the trolleys.

There were some glorious moments for African Americans in this period as well. In 1870, Richard T. Greener, a brilliant native of Philadelphia, became the first African American to graduate from Harvard University. Six years later, the eyes of the world were focused on

Philadelphia when the city hosted the centennial celebration in Fairmont Park. The centennial was the most extensive and the grandest ever held in the United States. African American artist Edward D. Bannister of Providence, Rhode Island, won one of the highest art prizes awarded the Centennial Exposition. A huge statue entitled *Freed Slave* attracted crowds of viewers.

In 1884, Christopher Perry founded the *Philadelphia Tribune*. From 1868 to 1884, Bishop Benjamin Tucker Tanner was editor of the *Christian Recorder*, while serving as pastor of Mother Bethel AME Church. His son, artist Henry Ossawa Tanner, noted for his religious, landscape paintings, left America because of the racism he experienced for Paris, where he earned international fame. In 1895, Dr. Nathan Mossell founded Mercy Hospital and became the first African American pharmacist in Pennsylvania. It was during this period that the American Negro Historical Society was founded and book collectors such as William C. Bolivar, Robert Adger, and William Dorsey began to build their collection of books and other documents by and about people of African descent.

In 1899, a brilliant scholar, Dr. William Edward Burghart Dubois, came to Philadelphia to conduct his scientific study of Philadelphia's African American community. He published his research in a book entitled *The Philadelphia Negro*. This was the first sociological study on blacks in the United States.

Freed Slave. Although they were confronted with discrimination, hundreds of African Americans throughout the nation traveled to Fairmount Park in Philadelphia during the centennial year of 1876 to view the statue of the freed slave. Shown is a proud group of individuals surrounding the monument.

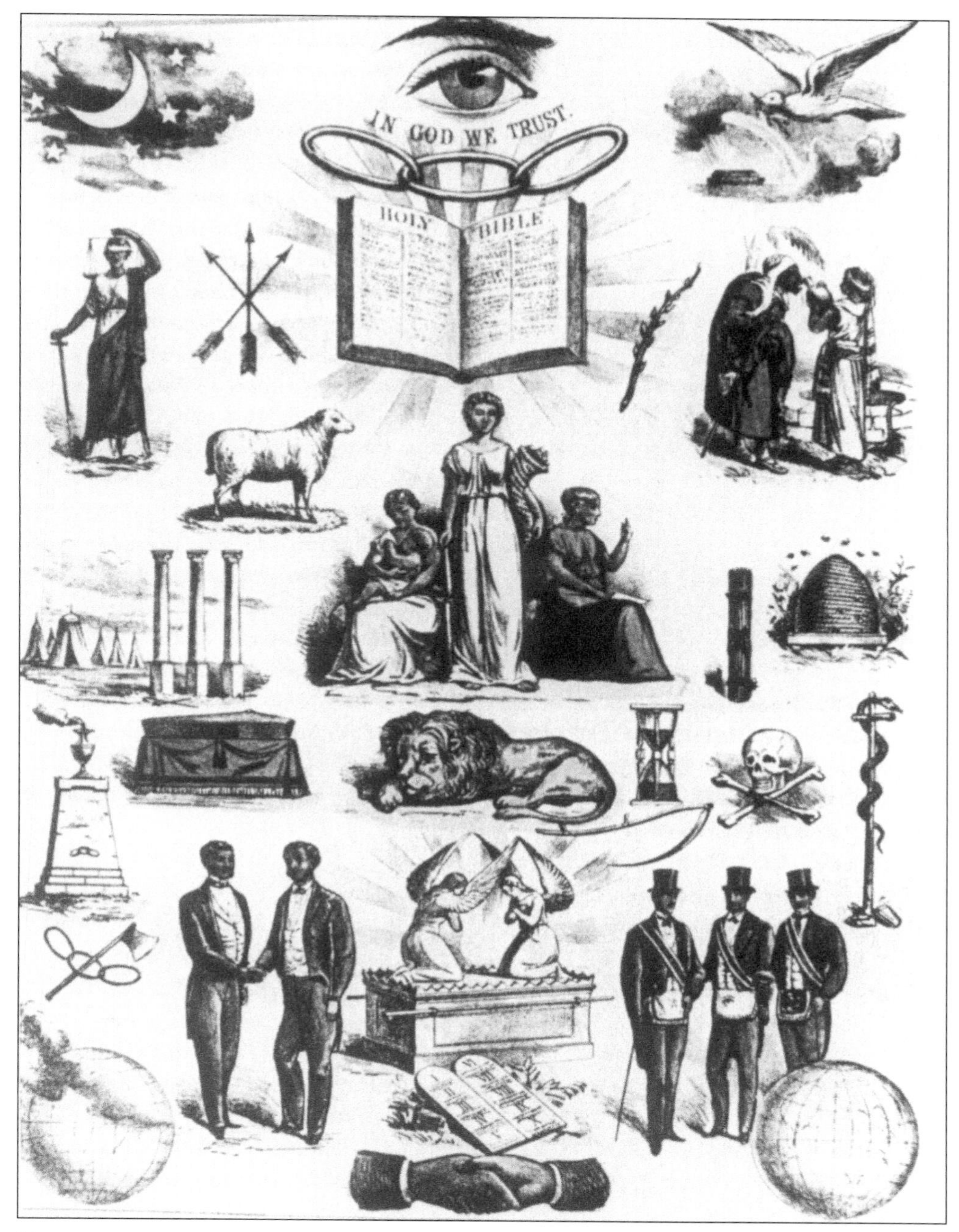

The Grand United Order of Odd Fellows. The Grand United Order of Odd Fellows was one of the largest fraternal organizations to spring from the community activities of the black churches.

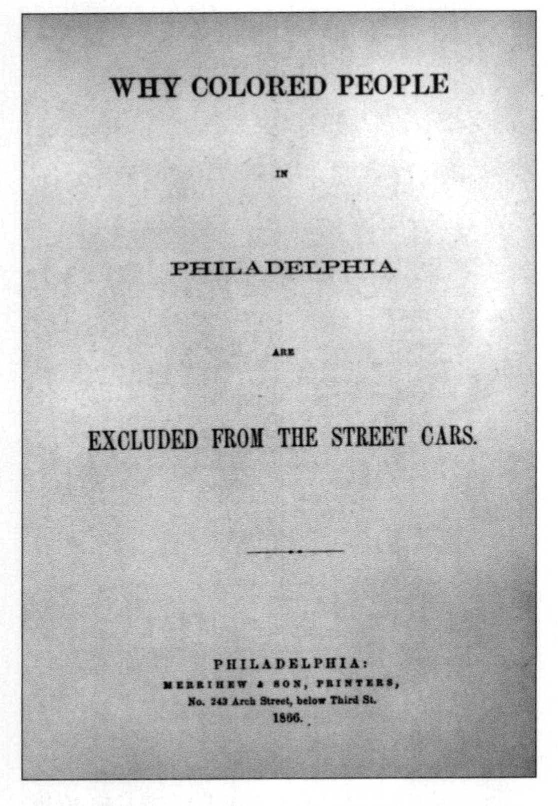

WHY COLORED PEOPLE

IN

PHILADELPHIA

ARE

EXCLUDED FROM THE STREET CARS.

PHILADELPHIA:
MERRIHEW & SON, PRINTERS,
No. 243 Arch Street, below Third St.
1866.

WHY COLORED PEOPLE IN PHILADELPHIA ARE EXCLUDED FROM THE STREET CARS. Several of the city's newspapers reported that January 7, 1866, was the coldest day ever in Philadelphia. The thermometer fell to 18 degrees below zero. Commenting on the freezing temperatures, one Philadelphia account stated that "this was no colder than the reception for the African American veterans of the Civil War, who found that they had been permitted to serve in the army, but could not ride a trolley in the City of 'Brotherly Love.'" Some newspapers spoke out against the exclusion of African Americans. Petitions to change the rules were signed by African American citizens and by a substantial number of white citizens. Nothing was done to correct the situation until the state legislature, not particularly sympathetic to African Americans, passed a law ordering streetcar lines to permit African Americans to ride along with whites.

FANNY JACKSON COPPIN. Fanny Jackson Coppin, one of the first African American women college graduates, began teaching at the Institute for Colored Youth in 1865 and was its principal from 1869 to 1901. She was also active in a variety of educational activities in the community and stressed the importance of industrial as well as academic training. She married Bishop Levi Coffin of the African Methodist Episcopal Church. Nationally known educator and founder of the Tuskeegee Institute Booker T. Washington adopted many of her progressive ideas for industrial education.

BISHOP BENJAMIN TUCKER TANNER. Born in Pittsburgh in 1835, Benjamin Tucker Tanner attended Avery College in that city and worked as a barber to pay expenses. He was later ordained a deacon and then an elder in the AME Church in 1860. In Philadelphia, he served as pastor of Mother Bethel AME Church beginning in 1868, where he was editor of the *Christian Recorder*, a church publication. Tanner was also a church historian; his most widely circulated book was a history of African Methodism, *An Apology for African Methodism*, published in 1867. The father of seven children, Tanner was consecrated a bishop in 1888.

HENRY OSSAWA TANNER. The eldest of the seven children of Bishop Benjamin T. Tanner and his wife, Sarah Elizabeth, Henry Ossawa Tanner was born in 1859. He began to develop a natural talent for art at an early age; he painted portraits, landscapes, and seascapes, and modeled clay figures. For a short time, he studied with Thoman Eakins at the Pennsylvania Academy of Fine Arts. Tanner arranged to go to Paris, where he lived a hand-to-mouth existence, selling only a few paintings. Tanner slowly won honors and recognition both there and in America. Although religious imagery characterized much of his work, Tanner's other works reveal his deep interest in his African American heritage. He was the first African American artist to have his work on permanent display at the White House.

THE CHRISTIAN RECORDER

GOD OUR FATHER — MAN OUR BROTHER

B. T. JOHNSON, EDITOR
.. C. EMBRY, PUBLISHER

PUBLISHED FOR THE A. M. E. CHURCH.

$2.00 Per Y

VOLUME XXXI. 631 PINE STREET, PHILADELPHIA, PA. MARCH 9, 1893. NUMBER

BIOGRAPHICAL SKETCH OF DR. C. S. SMITH, AND RESOLUTION OF RESPECT.

Dear Bishop B. W. Arnett and brethren of Middle Mississippi Annual Conference:—

We your committee on Biographical sketches and resolutions of respect, to whom were referred the pleasant duty of writing up such papers for presentation to your honorable body out of respect for Dr. C. S. Smith, general manager of the Sunday School Union, beg your indulgence to make the following report:

The committee find that Dr. C. S. Smith entered the State of Mississippi in the summer of 1871, and soon thereafter began teaching school. He taught first at Greenwood, Mississippi, secondly at Yazoo city, the present seat of your conference, and subsequently at several other places in the State—notably, Meridian.

In the spring of 1872, Dr. Smith joined the A. M. E. Church at Jackson, said church then being under the pastoral charge of Rev. O. A. Douglass.

The first quarterly conference following Dr. Smith's connection with the church licensed said gentleman to exhort; the second to preach, and the third recommended him to the annual conference for admission as an itinerant minister. Said annual [illegible] Dec. 1871.

Rt. Rev. T. M. D. Ward, D. D., presided. Dr. Smith was received into the connection. His first appointment was the Raymond Mission. According to reports made by the good people over whom he was placed, there was no lack of zeal on the part of young preacher Smith; for it is said that his labors were crowned with success.

Dr. Smith in his early ministerial calling seemed to have felt keenly the importance of his mission, so he soon transferred from the State of Mississippi and joined himself to the same work in other Episcopal Districts, first in the East then in the West, adding as he went success to success.

It was Dr. Smith who in 1882 suggested to the Honorable Board of Bishops the project of establishing what is known as the Sunday School Union of our Church. Those venerable fathers readily saw what great and lasting good might come to the entire connection from such an institution, and they said to Dr. Smith, "Do the work, you have our full consent and shall receive our hearty support and co-operation."

By the doctor's zeal and untiring efforts the Sunday School Union has made a reality; for to-day we have a building in the city of Nashville, Tenn., which cost five thousand dollars, to say nothing of the costly machinery, fixtures, and the hundreds of dollars worth of Sunday School literature.

The Sunday School Union Building is the Connection's pride, and that Dr. Smith's name is immortal

WHEREAS, This noble Christian gentleman and wise builder, Dr. C. S. Smith, has done so much as a general officer of the A. M. E. Church connection, and

WHEREAS, The whole Connection, as well as the Bishop and brethren of Mississippi, North Mississippi, and the Middle Mississippi conferences, have in [illegible] faithful son and true brother: therefore be it

Resolved: That the Middle Mississippi annual conference, now in session in Yazoo city, Miss., tender Dr. Smith a rising vote of thanks for his friendly visit and words of advice and accord him its continued prayer for his perfect safety and satisfactory success in his contemplated visit to Africa and exploration of the Congo Free States.

Be it further Resolved: That the conference, brethren and friends present be given an opportunity to show their great appreciation for Dr. Smith, by making him a freewill offering of whatever amount they will to aid him in his proposed African trip.

And be it further Resolved; That a copy of this biographical sketch and resolutions be spread upon the conference minutes and that a second be presented to Rev. Dr. Smith, as a small token of the high esteem with which he is held by the Bishop and members of the Middle Mississippi annual conference.

Respectfully submitted
W. T. STRINGER, Chairman,
W. T. DANGERFIELD,
O. A. DOUGLASS,
A. B. PATSON, Sec'y,
Committee.

Amount voted by conf. . $10 00
Amount presented by the brethren and friends. . . 5 15

Total amt. given. . . $15 15

MY FIRST TOUR [illegible]

BY A. S. JACKSON, P. E.

MR. EDITOR:—

At the close of the 20th annual session of the North Georgia annual conference, Rt. Rev. A. Grant, D. D., the staunch and all-around Bishop, and the greatest revivalist that lives in this age of the A. M. E. Church: whose executive ability is so profound, and dignified, re-appointed me to the presiding eldership of the Monticello District,—this being my third year.

A new influence is arising among my men, which is sufficiently able to supply the deficiencies of government, in attaining ends which they cannot reach otherwise. The boys know that marching must be done.

On the 23rd of Nov. 1892, we boarded the train at Cartersville, with every prospect of a comfortable passage. Though the iron horse fixed on steel rails, traveled at the rate of 31 miles an hour, the rumbling wheels could be heard at times like low thunder. But we rode on quietly to Monticello.

I entered the battle field, found my men at their post fixing up their business, and preparing for marching; for the Bishop has declared that marching must be done, and these soldiers for Christ, shepherds of His flock, have promised to further the great and grand old church work both spiritually and financially. They say all moneys must go beyond the previous years.

After we organized this year, with only two new men on the district, I had no watchword to give, for Bishop Grant had already given the watchword. By this we hope to land up next November at Marietta with a report that will please the Lord; and certainly if it goes beyond '92 the Bishop and conference will be pleased. Brethren, the way to do this is to be good husbands to your flocks, and success will be yours.

Now we move off with the work trying to note every foot of the way to and from. Though this has been the coldest winter we have had in fifteen or sixteen years, yet I have traveled 2,442 miles, railway and across country, preached 34 sermons, and lectured 5 times on Christian Education. We also found 2,388 members, and 190 probationers. With this number of incorporated Christian soldiers committed to the pastoral care of sixteen true ministers, we trust for great results.

Monticello Circuit.—Rev. J. A. Lindsey, the pastor, is doing a grand work. He is greatly beloved by his people. He is cancelling the debt on the church. He has a loyal people, and they say by the second quarter they will be very near out of debt. They raised Christmas, one hundred and twenty-five dollars. God bless the young man.

Madison Station.—Rev. R. D. Stinson, the pastor, is an earnest young man, who is very stable, with a strong will. He was heartily received by the people of Madison. With warm hearts they met him and his good lady. The members took right hold of him, and he says with the enthusiasm the people now have he will raise eight hundred or a thousand dollars this year. I can say they have made a good start. At the first quarter the trustees reported $128.

Coving[illegible], Rev. R. T. Matt[illegible]—This young man is [illegible] for bravery. Although this [illegible] fourth year, he can, [illegible] greater work than previ[illegible] years. As this is the seat of the District conference and Sunday School convention which will meet July 5th, he and his good people will build us a good church there for that purpose. Pray for them.

Conyers Station, the Rev. S. M. Alexander pastor, is our Daniel for increasing in favor. He was received by the members, and friends, of Conyers with gratitude that does not characterize every congregation. He and his good people are preparing to re-pew the church, and to build a steeple for the bell by the second quarter. Success to them.

Greensboro Station, Rev. A. G. Gonickey pastor, and our Hosea for faithfulness in dispensing the Lord's message. This is his fourth year, and he feels at home with his good people; although he labored very hard this year, he says he will still march in the crowd.

Jasper County Circuit, Rev. S. J. West pastor.—He is our Sam Jones for wit and technicality. This is his fourth year also, yet he still holds his own in the congregation. He and his good people have decided to ceil the church at Sun Flower, and Kings chapel also. We hope they may be successful in his last year's work.

Starrsville Circuit, Rev. W. H. Mance pastor. He is our historical preacher, and the Abraham for faithfulness. He and his good people think of building at Poppler's Hill. They are a good loyal people and will move at the tap of the old drum. Pray for their success.

Walton County Circuit, Rev. J. A. Johnson pastor.—There is something very peculiar about him. He is very winning, and generally carries his people. He has done more at this circuit than any one, and if the Secretary of the Church Extension society would let him have $50 or $50 he could get us a good church in that place. We certainly need one there.

White Plain Circuit, Rev. W. A. [illegible] for warring. He and his people are doing a grand work on that circuit. They are building a schoolhouse on the church lot. He has the lumber to build another room to the parsonage, and they have raised money enough to buy a lot in Siloam, where they are fixing to move St. Paul church.

New Bethel Circuit, Rev. J. T. Addie pastor.—This is our young hero and builder. He has built a parsonage since conference, and he is remodeling the church at New Bethel and is covering the church at Pine Grove. This was going on at my first quarter. He will lead his people to success.

Rutledge Circuit, Rev. L. Baxter pastor.—Like Peter, ready and quick, he and his good people will rebuild the church at Harmonie. He says we must march.

Pleasant Hill Circuit, Rev. J. C. Cash, pastor.—He is a remarkable young man, and is destined to become one of our leading elements in the church. God bless him and his good people.

Hillsboro Mission, Rev. G. W. Moland pastor.—This is his fourth year at this point. He has built a good church at this place 30x40. With 28 members, and friends, it is hoped they will finish this year.

Bushhead Mission, Rev. H. Redd pastor.—One of the old fathers in the conference, we wish him a successful year in his field.

Oxford Mission, the Rev. Grant Hawkins, pastor—Although this young man is in school, he feels if he could get some little help from somewhere, he could build us a church in Oxford, which we need in that place.

Now brethren; let me close with a word to you, what a man soweth that shall he reap. Do not wet your own powder, if you have preached a poor sermon, say nothing. It may not have been detected by the congregation. Do not tell your troubles. If some brother antagonizes, leave it for him to publish. Do not throw your difficulties out of the window. They will get out of the door as soon as you are able to meet them on the public square.

Do not preach your doubts, you are sure of enough in the Bible to preach about for a life-time. When you preach personal experience you come to Christ's formula, verily, verily, I say unto you, when you preach doubts or hersays, it is not you, but somebody else, that preaches and so it is not evidence that is accepted by the court of the judgments. If you have only doubts, quit preaching. Only conviction generate conviction. Do not critise your predecessor. He has friends and they will throw him at you. "With what judgment ye judge, ye shall be judge."

Do not quote your last charge, let the dead bury their dead. Some suggestion can follow the above cautions. You are forming a new partnership for righteousness, in which each is to see how much each can do for God. It is not what you can get out of them for yourself, but what you can get them to help do for the cause. Seek to so preach that men will desire to hear you. Popularity is not a sin. We have heard some men, believing themselves to be great, denounce every preacher who the church was ever anxious to hear. They exhibit their own great ability by the power with which they squeeze the juice out of their own production. If you have great ability you are

Now concerning the vote o[n] organic union. My quarterly [con]ference voted unanimously o[n] union; but they say, for God's [sake] don't change the grand old [name]. They say the Church is too s[trong] and the title A. M. E. has stoo[d too] long to change. They will tel[l you] we are for the union if you l[et the] name stand African Methodist [Epis]copal Church.

SECOND EPISCOPAL DIS[TRICT] ATTENTION.

To the Ministers, Members [and] Friends of the African Meth[odist] Episcopal Church, composing [the] Second Episcopal District.

My dear fellow laborers:—

This is to call your especial at[ten]tion to the Missionary collec[tion] which is to be observed on E[aster] Sabbath, April 2nd, 1893. I[t is] very important that each min[ister] endeavor to make this the most [suc]cessful missionary collection in [the] history of our Church. Our H[ome] and Foreign Missions demand[s] [illegible]

The law requires that fifty [per] cent of this money be sent to [Rev.] W. B. Derrick, D. D., Correspo[nd]ing Secretary of the Mission[ary Society] and the sixty per cent to be retai[ned] by the annual conference.

I fully concur with the sentim[ents] of Bishop D. A. Payne respect[ing] the rights of the annual confere[nce] to appropriate the sixty per cent [as] well as the forty per cent, if t[illegible] sions. It will show that a de[illegible] feeling is growing in our hearts [illegible] Foreign mission and a more lib[eral] spirit for the cause which Chr[ist] represents. You are required [by] the law to consecrate the whole d[ay] both in church and Sunday Scho[ol] on that day, to the cause of M[is]sions.

The Virginia conference will m[eet] April 12th, 1893, and the Baltim[ore] conference April 26th, 1893.

Dear brethren, it is very impo[rt]ant that we do our very best in t[he] collection of our Dollar mon[ey]. Everyone seem to be watching a[nd] waiting to see what the results [of] these two conferences will be. [I] am very anxious that they be t[he] most pleasant and profitable th[at] you ever experienced. Let us [all] pray for that end.

I find that the spiritual work [in] the churches is very encouragin[g]. The members of the most importa[nt] churches are asking for ministe[rs] who can preach with spiritual pow[er] and the ability of raising mon[ey] and to pay the indebtedness of t[he] churches. The men who can d[o] this kind of work are in deman[d] and circumstances will force the[m] into these appointments; therefo[re] let every man show himself a work[man] approved of God.

Fraternally yours,
W. J. GAINES.

DREDGING CONTRACTS AWARDED.

The Board of Port Wardens yes[terday] awarded the contracts fo[r] dredging docks on the Delawar[e] and Schuylkill into which sewer[s] empty, to the American Dredgin[g] Company, whose bid was 19 cent[s] a cubic foot, measured in scows.

Master Warden Ross called th[e] attention of the Board to the fact that Delaware pilots had been illegally cruising in Pennsylvania waters, and a resolution was adopted that no pilot holding a license from another State be allowed to cruise or be attached to any of the

The *Christian Recorder*. Shown is a copy of the 1893 edition of the *Christian Recorder*. Originally edited by Martin R. Delany of Pittsburgh, who called it the *Mystery*, the paper was later sold to the African Methodist Episcopal Church headquartered in Philadelphia.

Rev. Matthew Anderson. Rev. Matthew Anderson was born in Greencastle, Pennsylvania, in 1847. He later studied at Princeton Theological Seminary. For many years, Anderson served as pastor of the Berean Presbyterian Church in Philadelphia. He also founded the Berean Institute.

The Berean Institute. The Berean Institute was established to provide African Americans with training in skilled trades when access to other institutions was limited due to racial discrimination. Berean Institute was chartered in 1904. A state historical marker is located at 1901 Girard Avenue in front of the present building.

Christopher Perry. Christopher Perry Sr. founded the *Philadelphia Tribune*, the oldest continuously published African American newspaper in the country. In 1884, he published the first edition of the paper at 725 Sansom Street. Today, published biweekly, the *Philadelphia Tribune* continues to be the voice of the city's African American community. Directly in front of its present building, located at 520-26 South Sixteenth Street, stands a Pennsylvania state historical marker. Pictured below is an early office building of the *Philadelphia Tribune*.

James A. Bland. More than 600 songs are attributed to James A. Bland. They include "Carry Me Back to Old Virginny," the official state song of Virginia; "Oh, Dem Golden Slippers," the theme song of the Philadelphia Mummers; and "In the Evening by the Moonlight." He was an African American composer of fair complexion who lived in poverty before his fame spread over America and Europe during the 1890s. He returned to Philadelphia to a life of poverty and loneliness and died penniless in 1911. There was no money even for a modest funeral or grave marker. Gov. William M. Tuck and the Lions Club of Virginia accorded Bland an honorary burial in the Merion Cemetery in Bala Cynwyd, Pennsylvania. A state historical marker was erected at his grave site many years later.

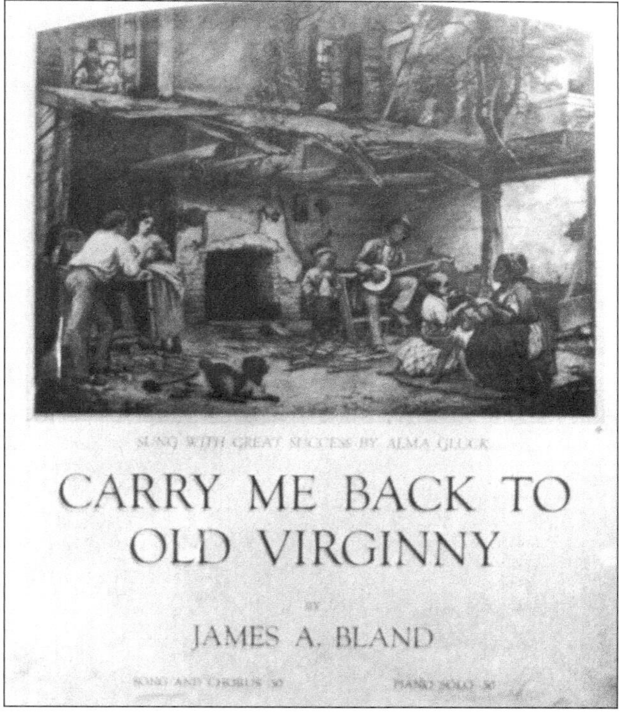

Dr. Henry M. Minton. Dr. Henry M. Minton was the founder of Mercy Hospital and the first African American pharmacist in Pennsylvania. He also founded the Sigma Pi Phi fraternity, commonly known as "the Boule" in 1909. This *c.* 1900 charcoal portrait represents one of the few surviving sketches of African American artist Edward Stidum, who was born in Philadelphia.

FREDERICK DOUGLASS MEMORIAL HOSPITAL. This was the first African American hospital in Philadelphia and the first hospital to be staffed wholly by African Americans. It was founded in 1895 by Dr. Nathan Mossell, one of the first African American graduates of the Medical School of the University of Pennsylvania. The hospital was primarily a training center for African American doctors, nurses, and pharmacists in a period when racial discrimination limited their opportunities in the medical profession. Fredrick Douglass Memorial Hospital no longer exists.

PHILADELPHIA—*World's Medical Centre*

Frederick Douglass Memorial Hospital and Training School

By ALFRED GORDON, M.D.

THE Frederick Douglass Memorial Hospital, first of its kind established in Pennsylvania, fighting an uphill battle from its humble start, has an enviable record of service to its credit. Founded in 1895 by Dr. N. F. Mossell, in a modest three-story building, located at 1512 Lombard Street, it has grown to a Class A Hospital, so recognized by National, State and County medical associations, with buildings and equipment modern in every detail and with a money value of three hundred thousand dollars ($300,000.00). The attending and consulting staffs of the hospital are composed of the most prominent doctors and surgeons in Philadelphia.

The hospital is provided with four public wards, a maternity ward, an emergency ward, a number of private and semi-private rooms, two diet kitchens, well planned and always kept under expert supervision. There are operating and sterilizing rooms and a special X-ray room for diagnosis with modernly equipped pathological and histological laboratories. The institution has 75 beds and at the completion of the Nurses' Home, now in process of construction, will add 25 beds, making it a hospital of 100-bed capacity.

No one is ever turned away from its doors because of creed or color, or because they are too poor to pay. Of the 4,531 bed patients cared for during the past five years, thirty percent (30%) were

Reprint from "Philadelphia—World's Medical Centre," authorized by Philadelphia County Medical Society.

COURTESY

IS A CREED AT MERCY-DOUGLASS HOSPITAL

★

HELP US ADHERE TO THIS DOCTRINE

"WHEN YOU AIN'T GOT NO MONEY, WELL YOU NEEDN'T COME 'ROUND"

"WHEN YOU AIN'T GOT NO MONEY, WELL YOU NEEDN'T COME 'ROUND." Published by a New York firm in 1899 in color, this advertisement appeared in the *Philadelphia Bulletin* as a Sunday art supplement. The illustration represents two African American couples dressed "to the nines." The style and class of Philadelphia's black elite was emulated by African Americans in other cities. In some quarters within the African American community and among certain white people, the terms of black society and black elite seemed ludicrous.

DR. WILLIAM EDWARD BURGHARDT DUBOIS. Teacher, historian, editor, poet, lecturer, author, activist, and pioneer sociologist W.E.B. Dubois was born in Great Barrington, Massachusetts, in 1868. In 1895, Dubois was the first African American to receive a doctorate degree from Harvard University. Dapper and urbane, he was one of the founders of the National Association for the Advancement of Colored People (NAACP). A state historical marker stands on Sixth Street to mark the site of Dubois's former home.

Publications
OF THE
University of Pennsylvania

SERIES IN
Political Economy and Public Law

NO. 14
THE PHILADELPHIA NEGRO
A SOCIAL STUDY

BY
W. E. BURGHARDT DU BOIS, Ph. D.
Some time Assistant in Sociology in the University of Pennsylvania; Professor of Economics and History in Atlanta University; Author of "The Suppression of the African Slave-Trade."

TOGETHER WITH
A SPECIAL REPORT ON DOMESTIC SERVICE
BY
ISABEL EATON, A. M.
Fellow of the College Settlements' Association

Published for the University
PHILADELPHIA
1899

THE PHILADELPHIA NEGRO. Dubois launched his career with *The Philadelphia Negro*, published in 1899, the massive study of the African American community in the city's Seventh Ward. *The Philadelphia Negro* was written while he was in the sociology department of the University of Pennsylvania and was the first scientific study of its kind. The study resulted in Dubois becoming the director of Atlanta University's Department for Studies of the Negro Problem.

The Old Banjo Player of South Street. This image shows an unidentified elderly musician seated in a chair as his banjo rests against the wall of his room. He is surrounded by all of his personal possessions. The photographer captured a legion of experience in the old musician's face. The photograph was found in a demolished home on South Street.

Five

The Twentieth Century: 1900–1976

In 1900, Philadelphia's population was nearly 1.3 million. By 1930, during the Great Depression, there were 1.95 million inhabitants in the city. At the turn of the 20th century, the African American population of Philadelphia was the largest of any northern city. In 1910, it numbered over 84,000, and by 1920 had increased by 58 percent. This growing population had many problems to solve, and the sociological studies of Dr. W.E.B. Dubois and others were essential to learn how best to respond to these problems. In fact, Dubois correctly stated in his 1903 *The Souls of Black Folks*, "The problem of the Twentieth Century is the problem of the color line."

The 20th century would eventually lay hope and struggle at the feet of African Americans. Early in the century, the former Institute for Colored Youth changed its name to Cheyney State College; Dr. Leslie Pickney Hill, a well-known author and poet, became the college president. In 1910, Henry W. Bass, a lawyer, became the first African American elected to the state legislature, serving until 1914. Richard R. Wright Jr., a graduate from the University of Pennsylvania, published his doctoral dissertation in 1912 as *The Negro in Pennsylvania: A Study in Economic History*. Wright later became a college president and bishop of the AME Church. His father, Richard R. Wright Sr., also a college president, founded the Citizen Southern Bank in Philadelphia to offer banking privileges to African Americans. Dr. Ruth Wright Hayre, Bishop Wright's daughter, became the first African American school superintendent in Philadelphia. But one event in 1915 allowed for more racist sentiment in the white community and a spirit of brotherhood throughout the African American community. When D.W. Griffith's film *Birth of a Nation* was shown in Philadelphia, the African American community joined African Americans and others throughout the nation attacking the film for its racial slander.

In 1917, hundreds of Philadelphia's men and women again joined forces and answered their call to duty. With the entrance of the United States into World War I in April 1917, African Americans hoped that their participation in the war to save democracy would end domestic hostilities against their race. However, in 1918, a race riot occurred in Philadelphia. Some historians stated that the riot was a result of the mass migration of Southern blacks into the city. The *Philadelphia Tribune* urged, "We favor peace, but we say to the colored people, stand your ground like a man." In 1919, when the war ended, African American soldiers throughout the nation were greeted home with racial violence. The NAACP strongly spoke out against the racial hostilities throughout its magazine, the *Crisis*, which was edited by Dubois.

The migration of blacks from the south to northern industrial cities that had begun in the 19th century continued in Philadelphia until the Great Depression years of the 1930s. But with movement within the United States, there was still discussion about emigration to Africa. Jamaican-born Marcus Garvey organized his Universal Negro Improvement Association in 1917 and announced as its objective the creation of a strong black nation in Africa. The organization became one of the largest movements by people of African descent in the world. Philadelphia chapters of the organization were considered one of the largest in the United States.

During the 1920s, Philadelphia had a significant number of African American men and women of letters who made their marks beyond the city's boundaries. They included Dr. Alain Locke; Jessie Fauset and her brother, Arthur Huff Fauset; Allen Freelon; and Nellie Bright, who was secretary of *Black Opals*, a literary magazine. Julian Francis Abele, a graduate of the University of Pennsylvania, became the principle designer of Philadelphia Museum of Art and the Free Library of Philadelphia. Marian Anderson began receiving rave notices as a concert singer. Paul Robeson, who would years later live in Philadelphia, became one of the world's most popular men of his race. Dancer and singer Josephine Baker and Ethel Waters also had a connection with Philadelphia as did singers Pearl Bailey and Billie Holiday during the 1930s to the 1950s. Rev. Charles Tindley wrote gospel music and had a large following at his church, Tindley's Temple. Father Divine was a religious leader and founder of the Peace Mission Movement. In 1938, Crystal Bird Fausett became the first African American women elected to the Pennsylvania state legislature. She also advised Pres. Franklin D. Roosevelt and his wife, Eleanor, on racial matters during World War II.

From the 1930s through the 1960s, a number of noted political, fraternal, medical, educational, and cultural figures also emerged from Philadelphia's African American ranks. These people included Judge Raymond Pace Alexander and his lawyer wife, Sadie; physicians Dr. John P. Turner and Dr. Helen O. Dickens; Dr. Wilbur H. Strickland, the first medical director and later head of surgery of Mercy-Douglass Hospital; Atty. J. Austin Norris; Rev. Marshall L. Shepard, recorder of deeds; Samuel D. Holmes, state legislator; Judge William H Hastie; Judge Herbert E. Millen; Judge Theodore Spaulding; Hobson Reynolds, exalted ruler of the Elks; and E. Washington Rhodes of the *Philadelphia Tribune*.

During WWII, black celebrities entertained service men and women at the South Street USO Club. Other more affluent African Americans representing "high society" organized clubs and sororities such as the Northeasterners, the Girlfriends, and the Jack and Jill Clubs.

The Cotillion Society, founded by Dr. Eugene Wayman Jones, loomed large in the life of these groups. One of the most active social and cultural organizations was the Pyramid Club, founded in the mid-1930s. Among the prominent African Americans who visited the club were Bill "Bojangles" Robinson; boxer Joe Louis; composer Duke Ellington; author and poet Langston Hughes; politician and educator Adam Clayton Powell; and Dr. Mary McLeod Bethune.

Despite the advancement within the community, conditions were still far from encouraging. In 1944, the Philadelphia Transit strike began when white motormen and conductors went out on a week-long strike, violently opposed to admitting African Americans to the transit Employees Union. The local branches of the NAACP and the Philadelphia Urban League supported the African American workers.

Philadelphia's African American community became increasingly active during the Civil Rights movement of the 1950s and 1960s. Dr. Martin Luther King came to the city on various occasions to speak at Rev. William Gray's Bright Hope Baptist Church and to participate in the march of Girard College, led by Atty. Cecil B. Moore. Black Nationalist leader Malcolm X headed the city's Muslim religious mosque. Rev. Paul Washington, of the Church of the Advocate, hosted the Black Panthers Party Conventions in his church in 1968.

Throughout the trials and struggles of the 20th century, African Americans in Philadelphia still enjoyed many social outings and gatherings, some of which remain popular today. The first Mummer's String Band parade was held on January 1, 1901, and has become a Philadelphia tradition. James A. Bland wrote the theme song to the Mummer's parade, "Oh, Dem Golden Slippers." He also wrote the theme song of the State of Virginia, "Carry Me Back to Old Virginny." In 1939, a number of prominent African Americans gathered at his grave site in nearby Merion, Pennsylvania. Included among them were musician W.C. Handy, John Rosamond Johnson, and Dr. Charles Drew, a leading authority on the preservation of blood plasma and the first director of the American Red Cross blood bank. The Philadelphia Clef Club of Jazz and Performing Arts, located on the Avenue of the Arts, is recognized as the first faculty ever constructed specifically as a jazz institution.

John McKee owned a restaurant at the Reading Terminal and was one of the wealthiest African Americans in the nation. Today, Delilah Winder is the owner of the popular Delilah's Southern Cuisine located in the terminal. The "Greek" Picnic is a popular annual event that draws national attention to the city. It has been held in Philadelphia since the early 1980s and attracts not only African American fraternities and sororities, but also the young people from across the nation. The Penn Relays was one of the most important events for African Americans from every walk of life, held annually at the University of Pennsylvania, Franklin Field. Trips to the beach at Atlantic City were another source of fun and relaxation. Although a segregated section of the beach known as "Chicken Bone Beach" was roped off, beautiful women could be seen "sitting pretty" in the sun on "glamour row." The first African American theater in the city was the Standard Theater opening on South Street, east of Twelfth, on September 8, 1888. It remained a traditional theater until 1934, when it became a motion picture theater. In 1912, the Keystone Theater opened at 937–941 South Street, but closed in 1934. In 1919, the Dunbar Theater opened at Broad and Lombard Streets with an all African American cast in the play *Within the Law*. In later years, the Dunbar's name was changed to the Lincoln Theater. The Nicholas Brothers of Philadelphia, called the "greatest dance team of the 20th century," performed at the Standard and Royal Theaters. Included among other African American theaters are the Pearl, the Earle, the Nixon, the Uptown, and the once popular Royal Theater in South Philadelphia, which has recently seen an interest in restoration. Wealthy music entrepreneur Kenny Gamble is leading a group of business men and women to restore the Royal Theater, following in the tradition of John T. Gibson, an African American who purchased the Standard Theater in the early 1900s. Whenever Gibson would hear of a good act in other cities, he would wire the performers money to come to Philadelphia.

RICHARD T. GREENER. In 1870, Richard T. Greener became the first African American graduated from Harvard University. He was an important historical figure in African American history. An educator, lawyer, librarian, consular officer, and leader of reform movements, Greener was born in Philadelphia in 1844. He served as principal at the Institute for Colored Youth and taught Latin, Greek, international law, and U.S. Constitutional history at several other institutions. Greener, in July 1898, accepted appointment as the first U.S. consul to Vladivostok, Russia. Greener and his wife, Genevieve, were the parents of seven children.

WILLIAM CARL BOLIVAR. Philadelphia has had a significant number of African Americans of letters as well as literary societies and book collectors from the 1820s until the present. Carl W. Bolivar was born in Philadelphia in 1844 to a family who called themselves "the O.P.," or the "Old Philadelphians" of African American society. His family was active in the anti-slavery movement and was connected with the Underground Railroad. Bolivar was named the "Pencil Pusher" because for 22 years he wrote a column under that pen name for the *Philadelphia Tribune*. A charter member of the American Negro Historical Society, he also assembled one of the largest collections of books and other documents pertaining to people of African descent. His friends said that Bolivar was a "veritable walking encyclopedia." Bolivar is shown here in his library.

BELLE DE COSTA GREEN. Belle de Costa Green was a towering figure in the rare-book world from the 1920s to the 1950s. She was the daughter of Richard T. Greener; Belle dropped the last two letters from her last name and passed herself off as Portuguese. She was described by her peers as a brilliant, attractive, fair-skinned woman. By 1909, she was the librarian for one of the worlds wealthiest men, banker and rare book collector J.P. Morgan, who assembled an important collection of books and art in his New York City mansion. Belle traveled first class to Paris and other European cities, purchasing expensive rare items for Morgan. She made numerous trips to Philadelphia to visit her friend, Abraham Simon Rosenbach, who was known as the world's greatest seller. Probably because of fear of exposure, Belle seldom associated herself with African Americans.

HENRY W. BASS. Henry W. Bass was a lawyer. He became the first African American ever elected to the Pennsylvania state legislature and served from 1910 to 1914.

THE SOAP BOX CLUB. Organized around the turn of the century, the Soap Box Club attracted listeners in Philadelphia, New Jersey, New York, and Delaware. They were known for singing spirituals, ballads, and folk songs. They competed with the Philadelphia Concert Orchestra and the People's Choral Society—two African American organizations founded between 1906 and 1917. The Soap Box Club gained wide recognition before it dissolved in the 1930s. From that period to the present, Philadelphia has been a center for the cultivation of music among African Americans.

Shown is St. Peter's Claver's Roman Catholic Church located at Twelfth and Lombard Streets. This church was used exclusively by African American Catholics.

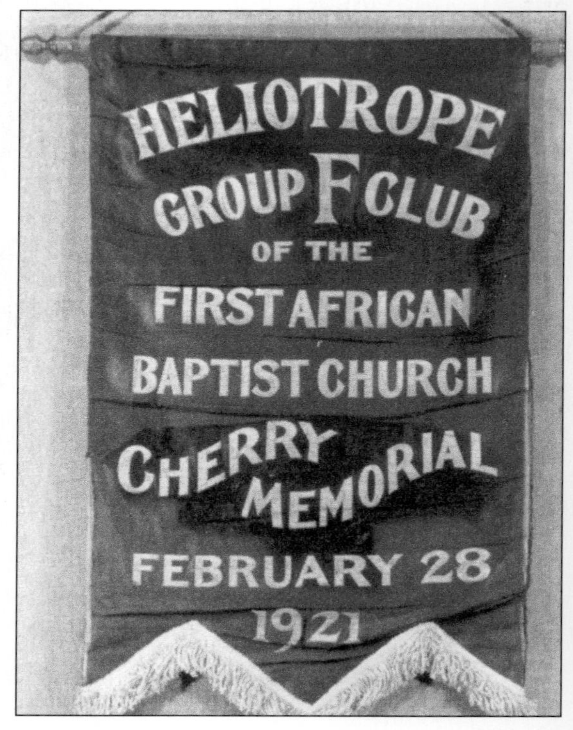

Silk Banner: First African Baptist Church. From its color and design, it is clear that this banner from one of Philadelphia's oldest Baptist churches is essentially a mourning piece. The banner's original purple silk measured 30 by 18 inches and was lettered in gilt. The banner included silk tassels at the bottom, affixed to a rod with brass ends in the manner of a Torah. The home of this banner was the original First African Baptist Church, an important stop on the Underground Railroad.

"Colored Man Is No Slacker." "Colored Man Is No Slacker" hung in homes of African Americans during WWI.

THE ALL WARS MEMORIAL TO COLORED SOLDIERS AND SAILORS. This large, inspiring monument was raised to honor Pennsylvania's African American servicemen who were killed in wars from the American Revolution to WWI. It was the brainchild of African American state representative Samuel Beecher Hart in 1925 and was unveiled on July 7, 1934. This imposing bronze and granite monument was designed by the internationally famed sculptor, J. Otto Schwetzer. The monument was originally relegated to a remote location in Fairmount Park. The Philadelphia Arts Jury and the Committee to Restore and Relocate lobbied elected officials to relocate it in 1994 to its current location at Twentieth Street and the Parkway.

MARCUS GARVEY. Marcus Garvey, a spellbinding orator, organizer, and black nationalist, was born in humble circumstances in St. Ann's Bay, Jamaica, in 1887. He was the youngest of 11 children. Shortly after he arrived in the United States, Garvey organized the United Negro Improvement Association. This organization became one of the largest mass movements among people of African decent in the world in the 1920s, stressing themes of black nationalism, racial pride, and a return to Africa. Although based in New York, the movement was adopted by hundreds of African Americans in Philadelphia, who were among its strongest supporters. Garvey's followers continue to hold meetings in the city.

FAMILY MEMBERS ARRIVING FROM THE SOUTH. Here, a newly arrived Southern family arrives in Philadelphia during the great migration in the early 1920s. The immigrants to the city in this period located overwhelmingly in North and South Philadelphia.

MRS. MARTHA B. EDWARDS

Capable Business Woman

MRS. EDWARD W. HENRY

Wife of President of Citizen Club and aggressive worker for Mercy Hospital.

MRS. CHRISTINA M. KEMP

School Vistor 34th Ward

MRS. MAUD M. MORRISSETT

A successful business woman and capa[ble] political leader of Seventh Ward.

MRS. BERNICE MORRIS

A successful business woman, who finds time to devote aggressively to Church and Sunday School work. In politics she is an accepted leader among the women voters.

MRS. E. C. BROWN

Wife of the country's foremost Colored Banker, and herself a Business Woman of extraordinary ability.

MRS. EVELYN ROBINSON

A leader in politics, who accomplis[hes] things where men have failed. In the 22nd Ward she is an acknowledged leader.

MR. AND MRS. A. B. COLEMAN

A congenial life partnership that's a big factor in developing the successful Coleman Realty Company.

Our delegates at the Bellevue-Stratford Hotel meeting of the National Council of Women's Federation.

Top Row, left to right: Mrs. D. A. Johnson, New York; Mrs. Sadie Carry, Oklahoma; Mrs. Maxie Mossill Guffin, Phila.; Miss A. M Jackson, Mrs. Ida Smith Wright, Phila. Lower Row, left to right: Mrs. G. E. Dickinson, Phila.; Mrs. E. Hunton, Indianapolis (representing Hallie Q. Brown, National President Colored Women's Clubs), Mrs. Ruth Bennett, Chester, Pa.; Mrs. Hunt, Georgia.

MISS ADELAIDE E. CREDITT

Social Visitor, Bureau of Constructive S[o]cial Service, Welfare Department.

MISS IVA BURR

Women Prominent in Race Activities During Past Year

Prominent Philadelphia African American Women Delegates. Delegates of the National Council of Negro Women's Federation met at the Bellevue-Stratford Hotel. The event took place in December 1921, as reported by the *Philadelphia Tribune*.

The Knight's Templar Band. The Knight's Templar Band performed at fraternal, political, and military events.

JULIAN FRANCES ABELE. Born in 1881 in South Philadelphia, Julian Francis Abele was educated at the Institute for Colored Youth. In 1902, he was the first African American to graduate from the University of Pennsylvania School of Architecture. Abele also was the first African American to have an impact on the design of large buildings in the United States. Much of Abele's professional career was spent with the firm of Horace Trumbauer. He became Trumbauer's chief designer and designed several well-known institutions such as the Free Library of Philadelphia and the Philadelphia Museum of Art. A state historical marker noting Abele's contribution is erected in front of the museum's famous steps.

CRYSTAL BIRD FAUSET. Crystal Bird Fauset was the wife of Dr. Arthur Huff Fauset. A social worker, educator, and politician, she became, in 1938, the first African American woman elected to the Pennsylvania state legislature. A graduate of Cheyney State Teachers College, she was the first African American woman to be elected to a state House of Representatives in the United States. Later, she was a member of Pres. Franklin Roosevelt's "Black Cabinet."

DR. ARTHUR HUFF FAUSET. College instructor, author, anthropologist, editor, civil rights activist, and school principal Dr. Fauset was the brother of writer Jessie Fauset and the husband of Crystal Bird Fauset. In 1944, he wrote *Black Gods of the Metropolis: Negro Religious Cults of the Urban North*, published by the University of Pennsylvania Press. In 1969, Fauset wrote a multicultural children's book—entitled *America: Red, White, Black, Yellow*—with another Philadelphia African American principal, Dr. Nellie Bright.

Jessie Redmon Fauset. Jessie Fauset was educated in the city's public schools and went on to earn a Bachelor of Arts degree at Cornell University (1905) and a Master of Arts degree from the University of Pennsylvania. She later studied at the Sorbonne. Today, Fauset is known as a novelist, a poet, a teacher, the literary editor of the *Crisis*, a translator, and a Latin and French teacher. The daughter of an old Philadelphia family, she was one of the most prolific writers of the Harlem Renaissance movement during the 1920s. Fauset attended Pan African congresses in London, Brussels, and Paris. She was also a member of the Black Opals, a Philadelphia literary group.

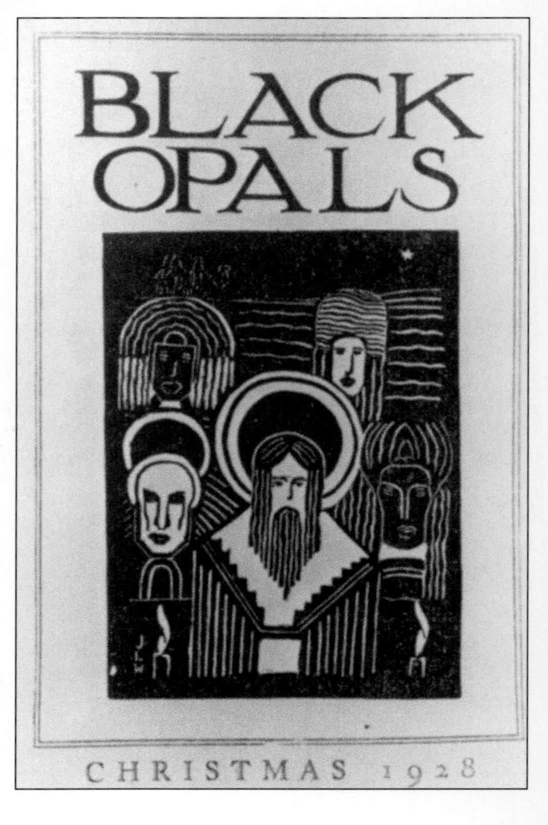

The Black Opals. The Black Opals represented the flowering of the movement known as the Harlem Renaissance that began in New York City during the 1920s. Members of the Philadelphia group published numerous pamphlets, including this one issued in 1928. Members of the Black Opals included Jessie Fauset, Arthur Huff Fauset, Nellie Bright, and Allen Freelon. Also among the members was Dr. Alain Locke, a native Philadelphian and graduate of the University of Pennsylvania, who went on to Oxford as the first African American Rhodes Scholar. Locke offered the group much needed valuable support.

DR. NELLIE BRIGHT. Dr. Nellie R. Bright, a brilliant, tall, slender, soft-spoken woman, made a name for herself in Philadelphia's educational and literary world from the 1920s until she died in 1976. Bright was the only child of parents from the Virgin Islands; her father served as an Episcopal clergyman in Philadelphia. Nellie Bright graduated from the University of Pennsylvania with a Ph.D. and contributed to the Harlem Renaissance movement as a writer and served as secretary for the Philadelphia Black Opals. She was also a world traveler and a school principal who was loved by her students. Bright was a member of the Pennsylvania Abolition Society for many years.

Josephine Baker. Born in 1906, Josephine Baker was born in Missouri in 1906, blessed with exotic beauty, flaming ambition, flashing eyes, and mesmerizing singing and dancing. Baker left her impoverished childhood and began a career as an entertainer. She captivated Paris like a storm during the Jazz Age of the 1920s and became a legend in her lifetime. Early in her career, she stayed at the residence of Mom Charleston when performing at the Royal Theater in Philadelphia and married the second of her many husbands, William "Billy" Baker. The young couple lived for a period during their short marriage at the home and restaurant of her her husband's parents at 1520 South Street. The building still stands. The photograph at left shows Baker in her scanty attire posing for a photographer during the time she was performing in Paris. The later photograph below shows her addressing a group of admirers at a luncheon held at the YMCA in Philadelphia during the 1950s.

Ethel Waters. Ethel Waters was born in nearby Chester, Pennsylvania, but grew up in Philadelphia. She began her career at age five and later won wide acclaim as a dancer, singer, and dramatic actress. During the Harlem Renaissance years of 1920s, she was known as "Sweet Mama Stringbean" for the way she danced the Charleston. She is remembered most notably on stage in as a cast member of *The Wedding* and for her Academy Award–nominated performance for the movie *Pinky*.

Marian Anderson. The beloved diva Marian Anderson was usually photographed in a stately and serious composure. But this image of the "Lady from Philadelphia," as Marian Anderson was called, shows her laughing, reflecting a jovial mood.

DUKE ELLINGTON AND DR. ALAIN LEROY LOCKE. In this 1940s photograph, renowned bandleader Duke Ellington (left) and Dr. Alain Leroy Locke enjoy a conversation at the Pyramid Club. Locke was born into an elite family and his entire life was associated with letters. After a brilliant record at Philadelphia's Central High School, he graduated at age 15. In 1908, he graduated *magna cum laude* from Harvard with a membership into Phi Beta Kappa. Locke was also the first African American Rhodes Scholar. He received a degree in literature from Oxford University in 1911 and studied in Berlin and the College de France in Paris. In 1925, he published *The New Negro*, which became the most important book of the Harlem Renaissance. Locke taught philosophy at Howard University in Washington, D.C., for over 40 years. He simultaneously served as chairman of that department until he died in 1954.

EAST CALVARY METHODIST CHURCH. The Reverend Charles Albert Tindley founded this church in 1902 as the East Calvary Methodist Church; it was later renamed in his honor. Reverend Tindley arrived in Philadelphia in 1870 to study the ministry. He became known as a composer of gospel songs and was instrumental in helping migrants from the South who had settled in Philadelphia. His church has a tradition of providing free meals and clothing to the needy. Reverend Tindley wrote the music to the soul-stirring civil rights song "We Shall Overcome." The church's organ is one of the largest in the United States.

SAMUEL D. HOLMES. Samuel D. Holmes, a south Philadelphia newsstand owner and businessman, served as a Democratic state representative from 1937 to 1940. Arriving in the city in 1920, he was a member of the NAACP and was a 33rd-degree member of Most Worthy Grand Lodge of Masons, and a member of the BPOE. His newsstand, Sam's Place, is a landmark meeting place at Fifteenth and South Streets. It also serves as sort of a museum, as the walls are covered with pictures of African American history. In this 1930 photograph, Holmes (on the right) poses with a friend.

A HOLMES FAMILY MEMBER. This 1930s photograph shows an unidentified member of the Samuel D. Holmes family.

THE *WINK* MAGAZINE ADVERTISEMENT. Published bimonthly and advertised as "Philadelphia's Only Colored Magazine," the *Wink* began publication in 1933 with an office at 1638 Lombard Street. The magazine directed its message at an urban, educated, middle-class audience with educational and cultural concerns. A typical issue carried several poems, occasional pieces of fiction, and a variety of advertisements. On the cover of this issue is an illustration by Philadelphia schoolteacher and artist Sam Brown, who was also a printmaker. Publication of the *Wink* lasted less than two years, from 1933 to 1934.

2 THE WINK

H. B. WATSON
Tonsorial Artist
Sanitary and Efficient Service
Chair No. 4
1513 SOUTH ST. PHILA.
THE

BROWN

PHOTO STUDIO

1408 South St., Philadelphia, Pa.

* * *

Photographs for Every Purpose

* * *

(Formerly at 513 S. 17th St.)

All Work Guaranteed

Social and Club News Published
FREE
in the
weekly edition of the
PITTSBURGH
COURIER

TUCKER'S
TEA ROOM
Stop and Eat With Us
And Enjoy a Home-
Cooked Meal
730 S. 17th St.
For Reservations
Phone: Kin. 3348

"Hats Men Like"
STRAW HATS, $1 and up
PENN
HAT
CO.
40th ab. Market St.

For Expert Hair Cutting
Individual Styles and
Creations
For Men and Women
See
MANUEL V.
BRUNET
DeLuxe Barber Shop
1513 South Street
5th Chair

* * *

Dr. H. D. Taylor
Surgeon Dentist

See G. L. WELLS,
For the Latest Styles in
Hair Cutting, Bob'ing, Expe
Massaging, Scalp Manipulation
Painless Shaving.
Care of the Face a Specialty

Second Chair
1513 SOUTH STREET
Polite and Quick Service
Our Motto

IN PHILLY IT'S
the
DOUGLASS HOTEL
1409 Lombard Street

60 Outside Rooms
with private telephones.
Single rooms, $1.50 and
daily; weekly, $7.00 and up.
Double rooms, $1.50 and
daily; weekly, $8.00 and up.
Running water in each room.

ARNETTE L.
DAVENPORT
Dressmaking
Lingerie Salon
Creations and Alterations

UNMARKED GRAVE OF JAMES A. BLAND. Featured in this historic photograph is a group gathered around songwriter James A. Bland's unmarked grave at the Merion Cemetery in Bala Cynwyd, on August 1, 1939. Also shown is Dr. James Frances Cooke, editor of *Etude Magazine*, speaking to the group. Another distinguished African American, composer J. Rosamond Johnson, who co-wrote "Life Every Voice and Sing" with his brother, James Weldon Johnson, is seated in the center of the photograph holding a white hat. Also in the center of the photograph is celebrated composer W.C. Handy (holding a walking cane). Handy, whose most famous song is "The St. Louis Blues," is acknowledged as the "father of the blues."

THE BOULE. Sitting in elegant style in an outdoor environment in the 1930s is a group of women whose husbands are members of Sigma Pi Phi, commonly known as the Boule, founded by Dr. Henry M. Minton of Philadelphia in 1909. This African American fraternal organization was for men of achievement and accomplishment, as well as professional and economic status.

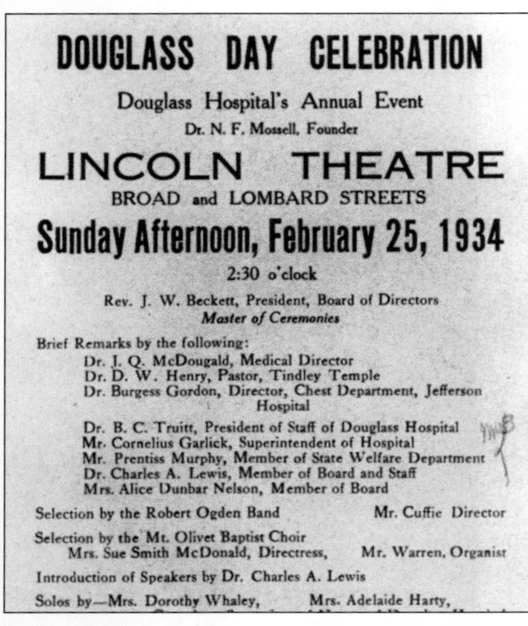

Left: **THE DOUGLASS DAY CELEBRATION.** This rare broadside commemorates the celebration of the annual Douglass Day, sponsored by the board of directors of the Fredrick Douglass Memorial Hospital. This broadside also includes the names of prominent members of the board of directors, including its founder, Dr. Nathan F. Mossell. *Right:* **THE DOUGLASS HOTEL.** The Douglass Hotel became an important place of lodging among African American visitors and entertainers primarily because of the racism and segregation associated with white-owned hotels. Nearly every important African American religious, political, and cultural personality who visited Philadelphia stayed at the Douglass Hotel from the 1920s through 1950s. Listed among them are Bert Williams, Ethel Waters, Florence Mills, Jack Johnson, Josephine Baker, Billie Holiday, Ella Fitzgerald, Billy Eckstine, and Philadelphian Pearl Bailey.

THE DOUGLASS HOTEL BUS DEPOT. Operated by African Americans, this bus company provided transportation along the eastern seaboard for individuals or groups of African Americans who wanted to take excursions or pleasure trips. The company made frequent trips to Atlantic City, Cape May, and Wildwood, New Jersey. In 1939, several buses were used to transport passengers to the New York World's Fair.

The Theaters. The earliest recorded appearance of an African American on stage in Philadelphia occurred in 1776, when an unnamed African American actor played a minor role in Murdock's *Triumph of Love* at the Chestnut Street Theater. Murdock also introduced the character Sambo to the American stage. The Nicholas Brothers of Philadelphia, called the "greatest dance team of the 20th century," performed at the Standard and Royal theaters. The Dunbar theater, once located at Brown and Lombard Street, was most famous of the African American–owned theaters until a fire destroyed it. The Standard Theater (on South Street near Twelfth Street) and the Lincoln Theater were also popular entertainment centers. Included among the white-owned and white-managed theater and movie houses that catered to African American audiences were the Pearl, the Earle, the Royal, the Nixon, and the Uptown Theaters. The Uptown Theater was eventually purchased by an African American firm in the 1970s.

Royal Theatre
South at 16th
WEEK OF JUNE 19th
Now! Matinee 15c till 5 P. M.
MONDAY
THE BIG DRIVE
AND
OLIVER TWIST
TUESDAY
TRICK FOR TRICK
Ralph Morgan, Victory Jory,
Sally Blane.
WEDNESDAY and THURSDAY
Raymon Navorro in
THE BARBARIAN
FRIDAY
HELLO, SISTER
James Dunn, Zasu Pitts.
SATURDAY
Lionel Barrymore in
LOOKING FORWARD

Royal
Theatre
SOUTH ST. AT 15TH
AMERICA'S FINEST
COLORED PHOTOPLAY
HOUSE
Showing the Finest First Run Photoplays
at Popular Prices
Children 10c at all times

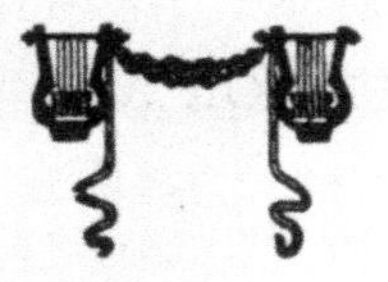

Standard
Theatre
SOUTH STREET AT 12th
SO. PHLA'S. POPULAR
PLAYHOUSE
Now showing selected Feature Photoplays and Variety Screen Novelties at Lowest Prices Possible.
10—15—20c
Children 10c at all times

Father Divine. Father Divine was one of the most fascinating religious leaders of the 20th century. Hundreds of his followers, black and white, filled streets, churches, and halls to become disciples of his worldwide kingdom of peace. His conviction and motto was, "Father will provide." Father Divine's properties included his vast estate, Woodmont, in Gladwyn, Pennsylvania, the Divine Lorraine Hotel in North Philadelphia, and the Divine Tracy in West Philadelphia. Father Divine died on September 12, 1965.

Austin Norris. Shown leaving the old Philadelphia Pittsburgh Courier branch office in the 1940s is respected and influential attorney Austin Norris. Norris, who served as attorney for the popular Father Divine, was a prominent leader and mentor to many young African American lawyers during his day.

The Wissahickon Boys Club. Shown is one of the first buildings of the Wissahickon Boys Club. This club was organized in 1907 and sponsored the first African American basketball team the same year. Throughout the years, the club sponsored a variety of athletic teams, which included swimming, bowling, boxing, baseball, and track and field teams. Prominent Philadelphia athletes such as basketball player Wilt Chamberlain represented the club. Note the cobblestones in the street located in the historic Germantown section of Philadelphia.

The Albanis Street Colored Homes. Built in 1938, the Albanis Street Colored Homes was built primarily for middle-class African Americans. The homes represent one of the earliest experiments in community housing in Philadelphia. (Courtesy of the William Penn Museum and Archives.)

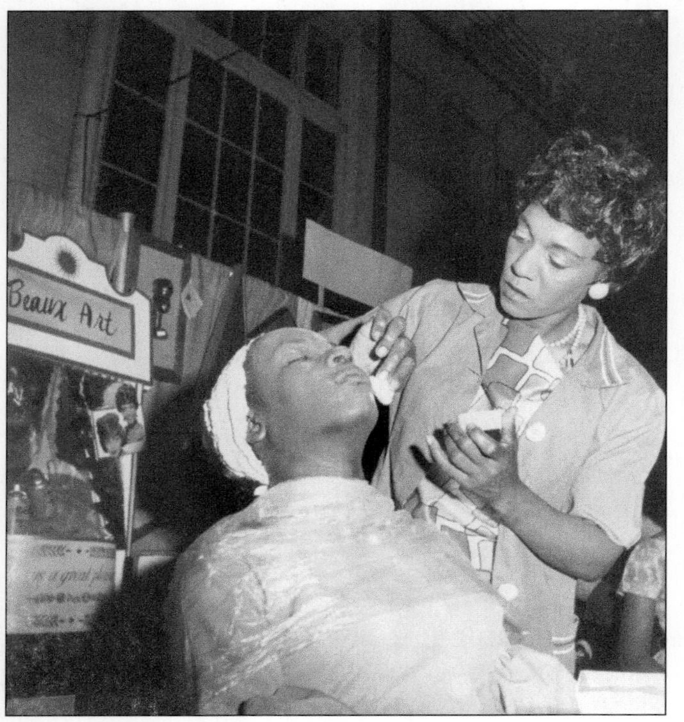

Apex Beauty College Students Preparing to Take a Trip. This group of young women students from the Apex Beauty College represented well-dressed college students of the 1950s and 1960s. At left, a woman sits with her eyes closed as she receives a facial from a licensed esthetician in 1955.

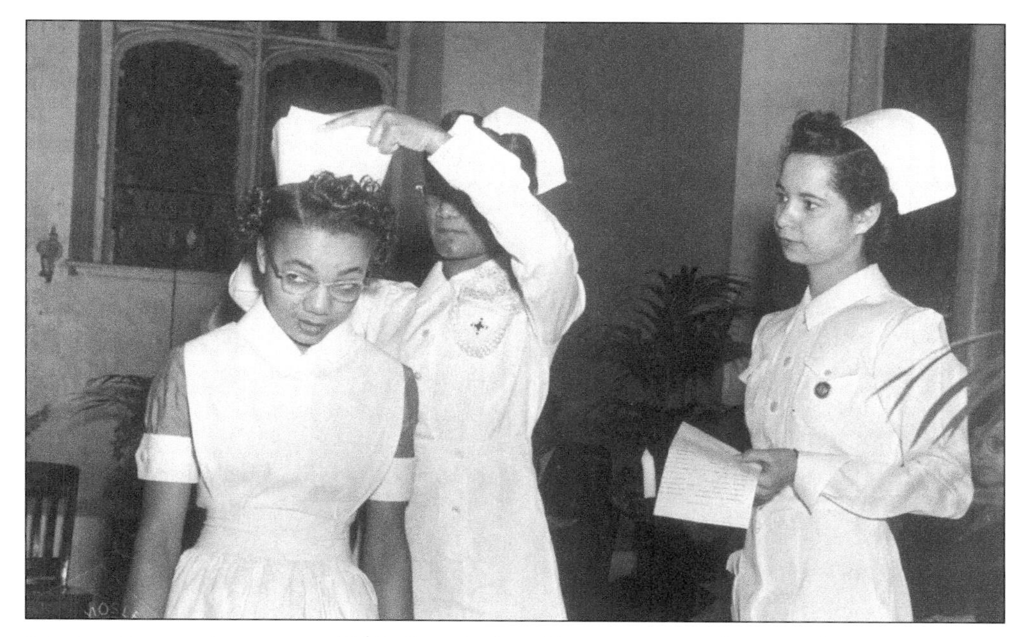

NURSES CAPPING EXERCISES, 1949. Proud Alma Thompson stands erect during a capping exercise of the Class of 1940 held at Mercy Hospital School for Nurses at Phillips Auditorium at 5000 Woodland Avenue.

MERCY HOSPITAL SCHOOL OF NURSING. Founded in 1907, Mercy Hospital School of Nursing was originally located at Fiftieth Street and Woodland Avenue. In 1922, Mercy Hospital housed a staff of 54 graduate nurses and had 85 beds. In 1930, the hospital acquired a modern nurses' home for $100,000 to house 40 young students enrolled in its nursing school. Shown is a student nurse ironing her uniform in 1936. (Photograph courtesy of the William Penn Museum and Archives.)

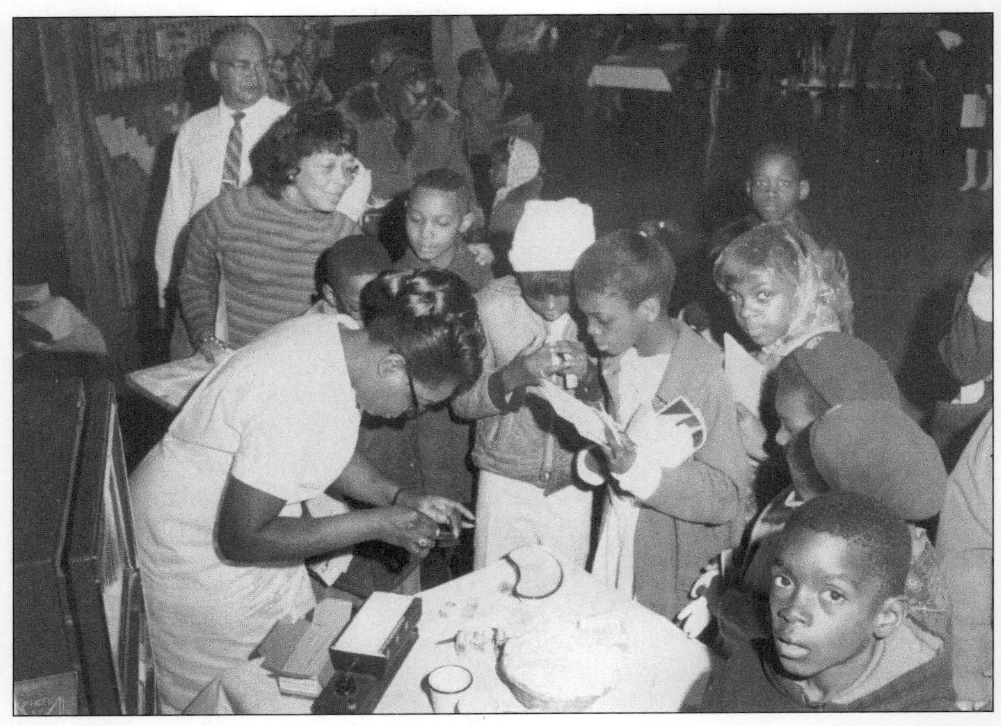

Student School Vaccination. Above, a group of frightened and curious young students anticipate their vaccination as school nurses prepare their needles in 1962. Below, another student receives health instructions from school teachers and nurses in the 1960s.

NEWSPAPER AND MAGAZINE VENDERS YOUNG AND OLD. At right, an elderly newspaper and magazine vender hawks two African American magazines while standing near his pushcart in the 1940s. Below, in 1948, a man stands holding a horn as three young boys are holding issues of several African American newspapers: the *Philadelphia Tribune*, the *Pittsburgh Courier*, and the *Philadelphia Independent*.

HOLLAND CATERING AND RESTAURANT. These remarkable photographs show both the exterior and interior of Holland Catering and Holland's restaurant. John Holland, through the 1930s and 1940s, conducted a thriving business in Center City, Philadelphia. After his death, William Newman operated the business and continued until his death. John C. Trower later purchased the business. The exterior of the restaurant features a stately, pleasant building. The interior of the building features an array of tables and chairs neatly arranged. (Courtesy of the William Penn Museum and Archives.)

BILLIE HOLIDAY. It is argued that Billie Holiday was unquestionably the most important influence on American popular singers of blues and jazz. Born in Philadelphia on April 7, 1915, as Eleanora Fagan, she was raised in Baltimore, Maryland. She was exposed to music as a child and was mentored by her idols, Bessie Smith and Louis Armstrong. During the 1930s, she sang with top musicians, including Teddy Wilson, and was vocalist with Count Basie and Artie Shaw. Two of her greatest and commercially successful recordings were "Fine and Mellow" (1939) and "Strange Fruit." She appeared on numerous occasions singing at the Show Boat and Pep's night clubs in South Philadelphia, often wearing her trademark white gardenia in her hair. While in the city to perform, Holiday often stayed at the Douglass Hotel.

The Pyramid Club. The Pyramid Club's motto was *Dum Vivmus Vivamus,* or "While we live, let us live." Founded in the mid-1930s, this club provided the African American community many of the social and cultural activities otherwise denied by a segregated city; it was thus the epitome of Philadelphia's African American elite society. Many Americans representing various races were invited to speak at the Pyramid Club. Although the club has been closed for many years, the building remains at 1527 West Girard Avenue.

The South Broad Street USO Club. Actor, singer, and civil rights leader Paul Robeson chats with a group of WWII servicemen in the South Broad Street USO in 1943. This photograph was taken while he was appearing in the record-breaking Broadway production of *Othello*. Robeson appeared before enormous military crowds in a USO tour to Europe after the war. The servicemen favorite songs were "Water Boy" and "Ol' Man River." Besides lending his support and performing at war bonds rallies, he appeared at labor gatherings, high schools, and colleges.

THE BEREAN MANUAL TRAINING AND INDUSTRIAL SCHOOL. Founded in 1899 by Rev. Dr. Matthew Anderson, the Berean Manual Training and Industrial School encouraged young people as well as adults to seek opportunities for employment through vocational education. Between 1900 and 1920, the school became the largest and most active of Philadelphia's private industrial schools for African Americans. Both Pres. Grover Cleveland and nationally known African American educator Booker T. Washington delivered keynote speeches at the annual conference of the Berean Training and Industrial School. Shown are two women concentrating on their sewing work in the 1940s. (Courtesy of the William Penn Museum and Archives.)

A HOME ECONOMIC CLASS, MEYER SULTZBERGER JUNIOR HIGH SCHOOL. In this 1940s photograph, young students follow their teacher's instruction in the kitchen of Meyer Sultzberger Junior High School. The school is located at Forty-seventh and Brown Streets.

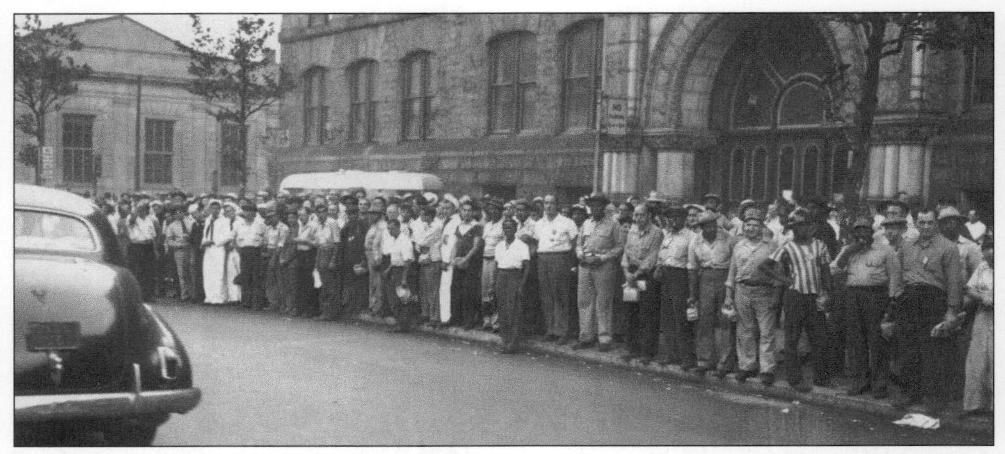

PHILADELPHIA TRANSIT PROTEST, 1944. In 1944, Pres. Franklin D. Roosevelt ended a wildcat strike of 2,000 white transit workers who refused to work with African American conductors employed by the Philadelphia Transit Company. The city was paralyzed while hundreds of defense workers who were employed during WWII were prevented from reaching their jobs. Black and white supporters held marches and other forms of protest against the Philadelphia Transit Company throughout the city. Some of the protesters carried signs representing Philadelphia's Fair Employment Commission. Above, a group of workers is prevented from reaching their place of employment because of the transit strike. Below, a white instructor teaches an African American how to operate the trolley car. (Courtesy of Temple University Urban Archives, Paley Library.)

PULLMAN RAILROAD CHEFS AND PORTERS. The Pullman Company and other railroad companies offered an important source of employment for African Americans. Many of these porters were college-educated, such as Philadelphia judge Raymond Pace Alexander, and became prominent leaders later in their lives. Other men were hired as chefs rather than dispatchers, engineers, and conductors during the 1920s through 1960s.

MOUNTED POLICEMEN. A group of policemen parades through an African American community in the 1940s.

The Gang's All Here. During the 1940s and 1960s, numerous neighborhood gangs controlled their "territory." Both boy and girl gangs fought to protect and expand their boundaries. Here, a group of gang members cleans a vacant lot while a supervisor looks on.

A Strange Place for a Car Wreck in North Philadelphia. This car came to a dead stop, demolishing the entrance door of an undertaker's home. Several young boys look on in amazement as if to say, "What happened?" The Upshur family has a long tradition in Philadelphia as undertakers. The family business continues to today.

YOUNG MAJORETTES. Pictured marching proudly in this 1940s photograph is a group of majorettes on a neighborhood street.

The Pin-Up Ladies. Photographer John W. Mosley took the photographs in this unusual collage of attractive women for a pictorial album of the Pyramid Club in 1944. Mosley took hundreds of photographs of beautiful African American women during the WWII era. Many of his pictures were sent to African American servicemen as pin-up girls. The models in the photographs were said to have been "sitting pretty."

AFRICAN AMERICAN MODELS IN THE 1940S AND 1950S. Today, African American models are known throughout the world for their elegance and beauty. However, during the 1940s through the 1960s, the world of fashion was primarily confined to appear in front of cameras on the runway in African American–sponsored fashion fairs, such as the internationally known Ebony Fashion Show.

JOE LOUIS, THE WORLD HEAVYWEIGHT BOXING CHAMPION. One of the world's most respected role models during the 1930s and 1940s was Joe Louis, who was born in Alabama in 1914. As the world heavyweight boxing champion, Louis was known as the "Brown Bomber" during his long boxing career. Louis visited Philadelphia on many occasions. Kneeling in a boxing ring at the Christian Street YMCA in 1940, Louis is shown with a group of young boys.

BASEBALL PLAYER ROY CAMPANELLA. Roy Campenella, a native of Philadelphia, was the first African American catcher in the major leagues. He asked the Philadelphia Phillies baseball organization for a chance to play organized baseball and was turned down. Campanella was three times voted the National League's Most Valuable Player as a catcher for the Brooklyn Dodgers. Early in his career, Campanella starred in the Negro League as player for the Baltimore Elite Giants.

Negro League Baseball Team Stars. Above, the members of the Philadelphia Stars pose before the call "play ball" is given. The team was part of the old Negro League and was owned and managed by Philadelphian Edward Bolden. Below, the famous baseball clown affectionately called "King Tut" is performing before the fans.

A Mother and Daughter Golf Outing. In a picturesque environment, a young child holds on to a golf club as her mother prepares the hit the golf ball.

Joe Louis and the Clara Ward Gospel Singers. The world-famous Clara Ward Gospel Singers stand around former world heavyweight boxing champion Joe Louis as he holds the Florence Mills Award, given to Clara Ward (third from left) and her sister, Willa Ward (far left), winners of the Pittsburgh Courier Theatrical Polls in 1953.

PRIDE ON MONTROSE STREET. On Montrose Street, adults supervise a group of children taking pride in keeping their block clean in July 1947. Community pride ruled supreme.

A SENSE OF PURPOSE IN THE NEIGHBORHOOD. This photograph represents community pride and patriotism in neighborhoods during WWII. Note how clean the streets are in both of the photographs on this page.

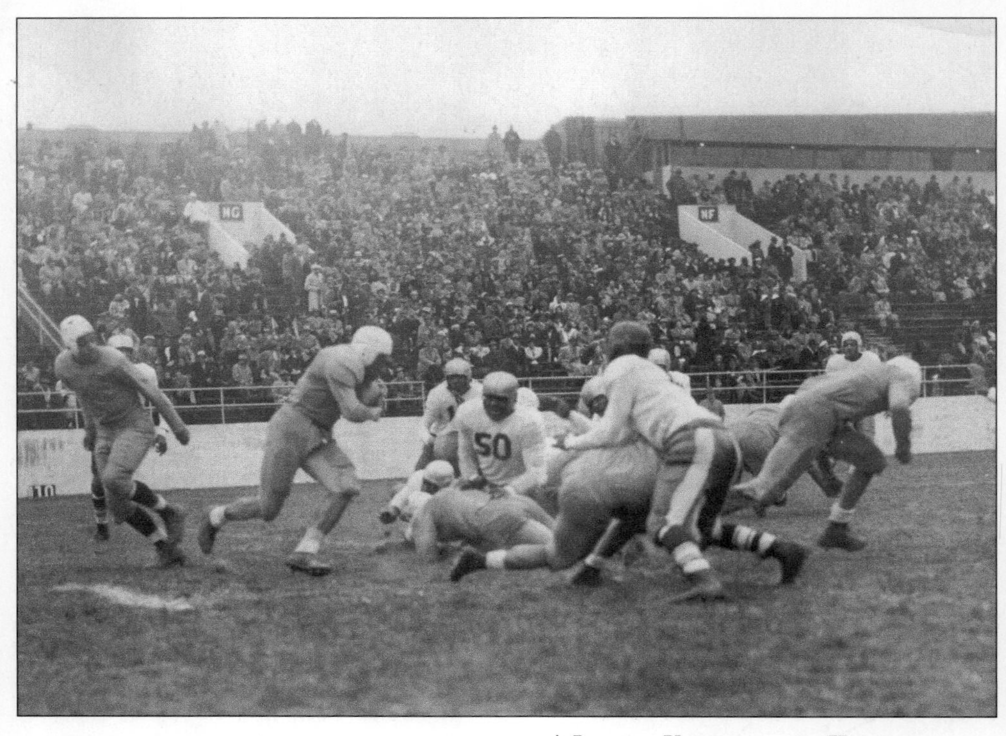

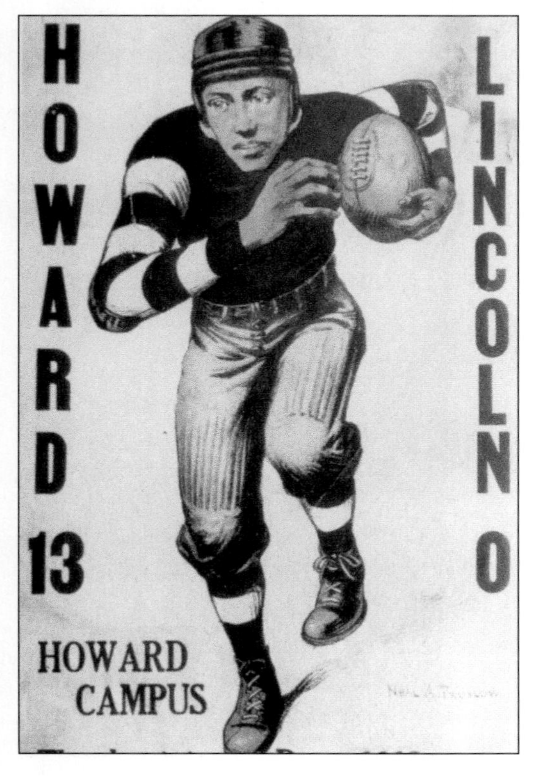

A Lincoln University and Howard University Annual football Game. Above, a group of fans watches the annual Lincoln University and Howard University football game held at Temple University Stadium in the early 1940s. The "Classic" series began in 1894. One attraction during the annual Lincoln and Howard University Thanksgiving Day games in 1912 was the illustrated poster shown at left. It was painted by African American artist Anna Russell Jones.

THE PROGRESSIVE PARTY CONVENTION, PHILADELPHIA (1948). The Philadelphia convention center became the site of national attention when the Progressive party held its convention in the city on July 25 and 26, 1948. Delegates from around the nation nominated Henry A. Wallace as their candidate for president of the United States. Many African American personalities participated in the convention as delegates and speakers. Actor, singer, and political activist Paul Robeson, delivered the keynote speech. Delegate Goldie Watson of Philadelphia was a well-known political activist and director of the city's Anti-Poverty Program of the 1960s. Watson was later appointed deputy mayor of the Frank Rizzo Administration in 1974. Another delegate at the 1948 convention was Coretta Scott, shown at right. Scott, who later married Rev. Martin Luther King Jr., was a student at Antioch college in Yellow Spring, Ohio, when she attended the founding convention of the Progressive Party Youth Organization.

MAJ. RICHARD ROBERT WRIGHT SR. Born in Dalton, Georgia, in 1855, Richard R. Wright Sr. was an educator, politician, editor, college president, and banker. Watson could trace his maternal grandmother, Lucy, to a Mandingo princess in Africa. At the age of ten, Wright and his mother traveled 200 miles to attend a school for emancipated slaves in Georgia. When Union general Oliver Otis Howard asked the classroom what message should he take back north, young Richard responded, "Sir, tell them we are rising." In Philadelphia, he founded and served as president of the Citizen and Southern Bank and Trust Company in 1921. In this 1940s photograph, Wright is entering his bank. The bank was located at the northeast corner of Nineteenth and South Streets. In 1992, the tradition of establishing an African American bank was continued when the United Bank in Philadelphia opened. It gave African Americans their first black-controlled bank in decades. Founder and CEO Emma Chappell is a native Philadelphian.

BISHOP RICHARD R. WRIGHT JR. A historian, educator, editor, college president, bishop, and world traveler, Richard Robert Wright Jr.'s distinguished career has often been compared to his illustrious father, Richard R. Wright Sr. In 1911, the same year he graduated from the University of Pennsylvania, he published his doctoral thesis *The Negro in Pennsylvania.* He edited the AME Church's *Christian Recorder*, served as vice president of his father's bank, served as president of Wilberforce College in Ohio, and was elected bishop of the AME Church. He also served as president of the Missionary Board in South Africa. He built 50 new churches during his term as bishop. Bishop Wright is shown seated in the second row, wearing a hat, watching a football game in 1934.

Dr. Ruth Wright Hayre. The daughter of Bishop R. Wright Jr. and a high school graduate at age 15, Dr. Ruth Wright Hayre was the first full-time African American teacher in the Philadelphia public school system. She also was the first African American senior high school principal and the first woman president of the Philadelphia Board of Education. Ruth Hayre completed her undergraduate work in secondary education at the University of Pennsylvania. She dedicated five decades of her life and much of her wealth to establishing a scholarship for city children called "Tell Them We Are Rising." It was named in honor of her grandfather, Richard R. Wright Sr. Here, Dr. Hayre is receiving flowers from two students.

Raymond Pace Alexander and Sadie Tanner Mossell Alexander. Both members of this nationally known husband and wife legal team were born in Philadelphia and were graduates of the University of Pennsylvania. Raymond Pace Alexander, also a graduate of Harvard University Law School, was the first African American to win election as a common pleas court judge in Pennsylvania. Sadie was the first African American woman in the United States to earn a doctoral degree, which was awarded to her by the University of Pennsylvania. Both husband and wife were active in the Civil Rights movement throughout the nation.

The Hungry Club. Attorney Austin Norris speaks at the Hungry Club luncheon as *Philadelphia Tribune* publisher and editor E. Washington Rhodes, wearing eyeglasses, takes notes at the table in 1948.

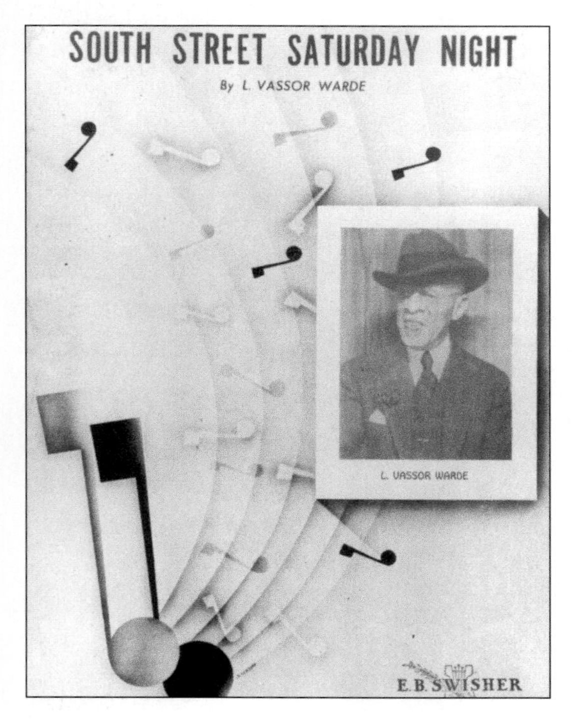

"South Street Saturday Night." African Americans had been living on South Street for nearly 150 years from the turn of the 19th century until the 1960s. South Street hummed with community pride. Professional men and women, mom and pop stores, travelers, shoppers, entertainers, athletes, laborers, and well-dressed celebrities suggested an affluence that no longer exists on South Street. When L. Vassor Warde composed "South Street Saturday Night" in 1944, the street evoked an atmosphere of street life that resonated with laughter, jive talk, and jazz. Two African American authors, William Gardener Smith and David Bradley, wrote novels about the street with identical titles, *South Street.*

WAITING FOR THE TENNIS COURT AND POSING WITH BALLOONS. Relaxing with smiles on their faces, family members sit on benches in the shade as they wait for their turn to occupy one of the tennis courts during the mid-1940s. At right, a picture taken during the early 1960s not only captures a family dressed in their Easter Sunday clothing, but also the background of tall city buildings, a pot of flowers, and balloons held by the children. The balloons advertise a local radio station, WIP.

MOM AND POP NEIGHBORHOOD STORES. African American–owned mom and pop grocery stores such as this one were an essential part of the city's African American neighborhoods from the 1940s through the 1970s.

THE WINGATE BEAUTY AND BARBER SUPPLY COMPANY. Wingate Beauty and Barber Supply was an African American–owned business.

A Record Shop. A group of young men and women poses for photographer John W. Mosley in a Philadelphia record store in 1948.

Nightclubs and Dinner Clubs. People enjoyed the nightclub scene in the early 1940s and 1950s. A number of these clubs opened as speakeasies during Prohibition in the 1920s and 1930s. The first nightclub to gain popularity after the selling of beer and liquor was legalized was the Sunset Grill, which later became the Showboat in South Philadelphia. Other popular clubs included the Parrish Café, the Moonlight club, Pep's Bar, the Harlem Club, Spider Kelleys, the Postal Card, and the 421 Club.

NAT "KING" COLE. Musician, singer, composer, and entertainer Nathaniel Adams Coles was born in Montgomery, Alabama, in 1917. Nat "King" Cole, as he was called, was one of the most beloved and versatile performers that this country ever produced. He was an important personality in the transition from the swing-era styles to modern jazz. His recordings sold into the millions. Listed among his most successful recordings are "Straighten up and Fly Right," "Mona Lisa," "Unforgettable," "Chestnuts Roasting on an Open Fire," and "Nature Boy." Here, Cole plays and sings before some of his Philadelphia fans in the 1940s.

ELEANOR ROOSEVELT GREETED BY CRYSTAL BIRD FAUSET. Eleanor Roosevelt (center) is greeted by Mrs. Crystal Bird Fauset (seventh from left), Marian Anderson (ninth from left), Dr. Horace D. Scott (far left), Bishop David H. Sims (third from left), and others in 1944. Eleanor Roosevelt had been invited to Philadelphia to speak to a group of influential Democrats.

A THANKSGIVING DAY DINNER DURING WWII. Neither the gloomy days of WWII nor the rigid division of Philadelphia's African American and white communities of that era could interrupt this family from enjoying their Thanksgiving Day dinner. The blessings have been said and a toast is being shared by all present. The African American family tradition continues today as the Philadelphia community celebrates the annual Black Family Reunion in Fairmont Park, where hundreds of families participate in a number of events, including tracing their genealogy.

A CONTROVERSIAL STATUE OF PAUL ROBESON. Antonio Salemme, a celebrated New York City sculptor, completed a larger-than-life statue of Paul Robeson in 1926. The nude statue stood for a year in the Palace of Legion of Honor in San Francisco and was highly appraised by art critics and others. In 1930, the Sculptors Committee of the Philadelphia Art Alliance asked Salemme to submit the statue for its annual exhibition held in Rittenhouse Square. After the nude state was submitted, the committee refused to accept the magnificent sculpture, stating, "the colored problem seems to be unusually great in Philadelphia." Sent to Paris, the Salemme statue was highly praised. Here, Salemme stands in his Greenwich Village studio in 1926 next to the nude statue of Robeson.

SCULPTOR ANTONIO SALEMME. Sculptor Antonio Salemme was 98 years old when he created this bronze bust of Charles L. Blockson. The bust was donated by Salemme at a ceremony held in Temple University's Sullivan Hall on December 5, 1990. Blockson stands on the left. To the right of the bust are Salemme and his wife, Martha. Noelle Blockson, daughter of Charles L. Blockson and curator of the collection that bears his name, stands to the right. Salemme, who died at age 102, had done earlier portraits of Paul Robeson, Ethel Waters, Pres. Dwight D. Eisenhower, and Pres. John F. Kennedy.

Charles Hicks Bustill and His Daughters. Charles Hicks Bustill (1816–1890) poses with his daughters, Gertrude Emily (1855–1947, left) and Maria Louisa (1853–1904, right). Bustill, whose ancestors were African, English, Quaker, and Native American, was a conductor on Philadelphia's Underground Railroad. His grandfather, Cyrus Bustill, operated a baker shop on Arch Street in Philadelphia. During the American Revolution, he delivered bread to George Washington's army at Valley Forge. Gertrude Emily was a prominent journalist and the wife of Dr. Nathaniel F. Mossell, the founder of Fredrick Douglass Memorial Hospital. Her sister, Maria Louisa, was a schoolteacher and the mother of Paul Robeson. (Courtesy of Lloyd Brown.)

The Bustills and Others. Shown standing inside a Philadelphia church in 1944 are members of the Bustill, Robeson, Mossell, and Alexander families. Shown, from left to right, are the following: (first row) Gertrude Bustill, Paul Robeson's aunt (wearing scarf); Mary Alexander (young girl); and Atty. Sadie Mossell Alexander, Mary Alexander's mother; (second row) Marian Robeson Forsythe, Paul Robeson's sister; Paul Robeson (with his hand on his aunt's shoulder); Gertrude Bustill Cunningham (wearing white hat); and Dr. Nathaniel Mossell; (third row) an unidentified Mossell family member; an unidentified woman; and Arron Mossell, Nathaniel's brother; (fourth row) an unidentified man and an unidentified girl.

HOBSON REYNOLDS. Hobson Reynolds—the son of a dirt poor farmer from North Carolina who raised tobacco, peanuts, and cotton—came to Philadelphia at the age of 19. By 1924, he was operating his undertaking business. Through hard work, his successful business expanded. By the time he was elected grand exalted ruler of the Elks in 1963, he was a wealthy and respected leader in the African American community throughout United States. Reynolds is shown raising his hand to onlookers. His car is driving along Broad Street during a 1963 Elks parade.

REYNOLDS'S FIRST FUNERAL HOME. This 1930s photograph, taken during the 1930s shows Reynolds's first funeral home, located on Ridge Avenue in North Philadelphia. Reynolds's favorite hobbies were tennis, baseball, and sailing with his poetess wife, Evelynn, aboard their 43-foot motor yacht, the *Evelynn*.

"Chicken Bone Beach," Atlantic City. Beginning in the 1920s, African Americans in Philadelphia and elsewhere along the eastern seacoast have been attracted to Atlantic City and its long, sandy beach to enjoy the recreational facilities. However, Atlantic City had Chicken Bone Beach, which was a roped, segregated area on Missouri Avenue for African Americans. That section of the beach received its name because of the many chicken bones that visitors left behind. Above, a group of visitors is crowded together on Chicken Bone Beach in the 1950s. The photograph at right, also from the 1950s, shows Club Harlem, a famous nightclub in Atlantic City.

The Philadelphia Urban League. Pictured in these photographs are members of the Philadelphia Urban League, which grew out of the Armstrong Association (1907). The Urban League was organized around the turn of the 20th century, along with the Association for the Protection of Colored Women (1905) and the Committee on Urban Conditions Among Negroes (1910). The Urban League periodically issues a report called *The State of Black Philadelphia.* The report covers various topics such as community wealth, neighborhood revitalization, and the amount of money spent annually by African Americans in Philadelphia. In 2000, the Urban League published *A Century of Greatness and the Urban League of Philadelphia*. They chose 100 African Americans who have contributed to Philadelphia's history and honored them throughout the year. These photographs were taken at an awards ceremony in the 1950s.

The First Colored Food Show, the Octavius V. Catto Lodge. Photographed in the early 1950s, these unidentified women pose in front of their display booths at the First Colored Food Show, which was held at the Octavius V. Catto Lodge. (Courtesy of the William Penn Museum and Archives.)

HOMES AND NEIGHBORHOODS. Located in North Philadelphia, the large home at right represents an example of residences owned by upper- and middle-class African Americans during the 1940s and 1950s. Below, several large trees lining a street in Germantown cast their shadow in front of middle-class African American home 1960s. Many prominent professional and middle-class Philadelphia families had summer homes in Cape May and Wildwood, New Jersey; Rehoboth Beach, Delaware; or Annapolis, Maryland. Those with more disposable incomes owned homes in Martha's Vineyard or Sag Harbor on Long Island, New York.

MRS. JOHNSON DIAMOND STREET DRESS SHOP. African American women living in North Philadelphia and elsewhere in the city found that it was not necessary to venture downtown to shop the large department stores such as Wanamaker's, Gimbels, or Lord & Taylor for the latest fashions. They found "acres of diamonds" in their own neighborhood when they visited Mrs. Johnson's Diamond Street Dress Shop. In these photographs, Mrs. Johnson shows customers the latest fashions.

The DeLuke Barber Shop, 1952. Barbershops have been a traditional part of the African American community since the early 1800s. Many of the early barbers in Philadelphia became wealthy by operating successful barbershops for "whites only." However, shops that catered to African American men and women offered a relaxing environment. These barbershop patrons usually had lively conversations pertaining to politics, sports, gossip, and the daily numbers or lotteries.

The Miss Sepia Beauty Contest. The first Miss Sepia beauty contest of Philadelphia was held in 1946. Many women in Philadelphia and surrounding counties sought the much coveted title. This photograph shows Miss Sepia 1948, Mae Madrid (sitting) being crowned by Helen Ritchie as the other contestants look on.

Beauty Contests. There were several other beauty contests sponsored by Philadelphia's African American community from the 1940s and 1960s, including Miss Ebony Pennsylvania. Smiling in this picture is Miss Ebony 1951, Deborah A. Oliver. Crowning her is Betty Fletcher Corbin, a former winner of the title. The terms *sepia* and *ebony,* meaning black, were used primarily by the African American news media.

BRIDES AND GROOMS. Happy couples pose for elegant pictures as they celebrate their wedding day.

A Rittenhouse Square Easter Stroll. Alice Christman proudly shows off her new Easter attire in the early 1950s during the annual Rittenhouse Square event. The square is located in the heart of Philadelphia, known as Society Hill.

The Purnell Family. While photographer John W. Mosley takes a picture of the Purnell family, young Randy Purnell focuses his camera to take a picture of his mother, Jennie, and his sister, Deborah, on Easter Sunday 1962 at Rittenhouse Square.

JOHN B. TAYLOR. John B. Taylor, a native of Philadelphia, was winning intercollegiate 440 yard track-and-field championships for the University of Pennsylvania as early as 1904. Taylor was one of the greatest "quarter-milers" in the world. During his collegiate years, he was the intercollegiate champion quarter-miler in 1904, 1907, and 1908. Taylor was America's hope in the Olympic games in London in 1908. However, an argument in a re-run race and interference by a spectator may have accounted for his failure to compete in the event, as Taylor and his American teammates walked off the track.

The Penn Relays. The Penn Relays, the oldest and largest track-and-field event in the nation, was established in 1896 by the University of Pennsylvania. Today, athletes come from elementary schools, high schools, colleges, and clubs from across the United States and beyond. The spectators are diverse and unique. Participants, old-timers, former fraternity brothers and sorority sisters, stylish dressers, party seekers, and others turn out to watch the events. Some people have been attending the Penn Relays for over 50 years. Some recall seeing Jesse Owens run before his triumph in the 1936 Olympics. Owens, who won the 100-yard dash in 1936, lost this race in 1935 to his arch rival and friend Eulace Peacock of Temple University. Below, five young women stand in front of the entrance to Franklin Field reading a 1945 Penn Relays program booklet.

GIRLS WADING IN A NEIGHBORHOOD POOL. Two unidentified girls stand in a neighborhood swimming pool cooling off from the hot summer sun.

CITIZEN DAY. This photograph shows a group of neighborhood children carrying handmade signs, posters, and banners, taking part in First Citizen Day in the early 1950s.

OPERATION GIRARD COLLEGE. The Girard College controversy began on May 1, 1965. Above, hundreds of protesters crowd the street in front of Girard College. At left, Atty. Cecil B. Moore and Rev. Martin Luther King Jr. raise hands as they stand on a platform in support of Girard College protesters in August 1965.

Girard College was the focal point of one of the longest legal cases in Philadelphia history. In his will, Stephen Girard stipulated that the institution would be for "poor white boys." The terms of his bequest were upheld for more than a century after the college was established in 1831. The case, however, was finally won by Atty. Cecil B. Moore in the 1960s, when he took the matter to the U.S. Supreme Court. During the period before the final ruling, the college was the site of a civil rights protest.

Prominent political and Social Leaders. Those shown, from left to right, are as follows: (front row) Judge William H. Hastie and Atty. Austin Norris; (back row) Hobson Reynolds, grand exalted ruler of the Elks; Rev. Marshall L. Sheppard Sr., recorder of deeds; and municipal court judge Theodore O. Spaulding. These men were listed as the most influential political leaders in Philadelphia's African American community.

Tanner G. Duckery. Dr. Tanner G. Duckery was was the president of Cheyney University and the first African American to be appointed assistant to the president of the Philadelphia Board of Education. Duckery is shown here talking to two students in 1947 from a Sulzberger Junior High School ceremony at which Dr. Duckery was the keynote speaker.

Social Clubs. Pictured in this 1950s photograph are seven members of the Girlfriends and the Links organizations, posing in smart and practical clothes for the summer. Both the Girlfriends and the Links were national women social clubs. Like other social clubs, such as Jack and Jill, the Links and Girlfriends sponsored affairs during the year, the proceeds from which were to help worthy civil organizations. Nearly everyone who had acquired social prominence wanted to be accepted in these organizations. Until recently, a code of color with high standards was the rule of the day. These so-called "blue veined" organizations on most occasions did not admit dark-skinned persons. If they could not pass the "paper bag test," that is, if the person's skin was darker than a brown paper bag, they were not permitted to join. Sometimes dark-skinned people were accepted if they came from a family of wealth or accomplishment. Several members of the Girlfriends were associated with other groups such as the exclusive Club GEACE, the acceptance in which required the proper lineage, along with fair skin. This national sisterhood organization still operates today.

The Junior League of Philadelphia. Shown is a group of young African American women representing the Junior League of Philadelphia. These young women were instrumental in assisting servicemen by organizing various activities for them during WWII. Because these women were not permitted to become members of white Junior Leagues, they organized the (Black) Junior League of Philadelphia in 1941.

THE NORTHEASTERNERS. There are many well organized African American women's social clubs. The three largest are the Links, the Northeasterners, and the Girlfriends. These prominent organizations have chapters in various parts of the United States, Canada, and the Caribbean. They give large donations to civic organizations, such as the United Negro College fund, the NAACP, and many national health organizations. Pictured in 1947 are members of the Norheasterners. Members of the Philadelphia branch of the Northeasterners hosted a major event in August 2000 in the city. The gathering included members from other states. The Philadelphia branch represents a legacy of achievement that reaches back to an earlier period of their social life, when their ancestors formed clubs such as the Bachelor Benedicts, the Society of Postal Clerks, the VVs, the Crescents, the Pequets, the Ugly Club, and the Olde Philadelphia Club.

THE OLDE PHILADELPHIA CLUB. This mid-1950s photograph shows one of the anniversary spring dances for members of the Olde Philadelphia Club. Their husbands and escorts surround the bejeweled women as they finish eating their midnight breakfast. There are a number of other prominent African American men's social organizations, such as the Guardsmen, the Commissioners, the Ashanti, and the Ramblers. The Guardsmen are made up primarily of physicians, lawyers, and prominent entrepreneurs.

The Jack and Jill of America Foundation. Established in Philadelphia in 1938, Jack and Jill of America was a dramatic response to racial segregation by 11 African American mothers of middle-class families to provide activities for their children. Today, the organization that was founded by Marion Turner Stubbs and Lela Jones operates more than 190 chapters throughout the nation. As part of its ongoing community service project, the organization's regular contributor to social service organizations including the United Negro College Fund and the NAACP legal defense fund. Shown is a group of older children from the Jack and Jill of America Foundation.

Mary Mason. African American media personalities have a long and rich tradition in Philadelphia's black community. Shown in this 1970s photograph is radio personality Mary Mason, whose name was Beatrice Turner in her early days. She has held her position as a popular radio talk show host for more than 40 years and has been influential in the community. She is affectionately called the "Queen of Talk Radio."

Philadelphia's Cotillion Society's Quadrille Dance Formation. The main dance featured at the Philadelphia Cotillion Society was called the Quadrille.

Marian Anderson. Marian Anderson, the acclaimed concert singer, was one of the prominent nationally known personalities honored by the Philadelphia Cotillion Society. She is shown here receiving a bouquet of flowers from Dr. Eugene Wayman Jones.

Dale Jackson. The lovely Dale G. Jackson is being presented to the court as her father and her unidentified escort assist her to the court floor at the Cotillion Society.

The Rocketts Women's Basketball Team. Women basketball teams did not toil in obscurity, as they did in many cities throughout America. Women's basketball clubs and teams were organized as early as 1931. The *Philadelphia Tribune*'s team were world champions. Among the team's stars was Ora Washington, who along with Inez Paterson was one of the greatest, all-around women athletes Philadelphia ever produced. In recent years, the city has produced several high school and collegiate stars, such as Dawn Staley, Shea Ralph, Tamika Catchings, and Shawnetta Stewart. Dawn Staley achieved fame as an Olympian and as a professional basketball player. Pictured in the 1940s are members of the acclaimed Philadelphia Rocketts receiving instructions from their male coach.

WILT CHAMBERLAIN AND JULIUS "DR. J" ERVING. Julius "Dr. J" Erving and Wilt Chamberlain revolutionized professional basketball while playing for the Philadelphia 76ers, with his shooting and his midair dramatics. In this picture, Chamberlain struggles for possession of the basketball with his arch rival, Bill Russell of the Boston Celtics at the Philadelphia Civic Center in 1963. Chamberlain once scored a record 100 points in a single game. Shortly before his death in 2000, Chamberlain was voted the greatest basketball player in Philadelphia's sports history.

A STATUE OF JULIUS "DR. J" ERVING. Julius Erving is regarded as one of Philadelphia's all-time beloved athletes for his abilities as an exciting basketball player and for his dignified, gentle manner when in the presence of fans.

The Dancers. Rooted in religion, African American dance in Philadelphia first appeared as a part of slave life and freed African Americans. Dancers, singers or bone players were often called upon to perform in various parts of the city, including Congo Square, now historic Washington Square. The word *dancing* conjures up memories of famous Philadelphia dancers, such as the world-famous Nickolas Brothers, Rhythm Brown, Bill and Pearl Bailey, and Josephine Baker. Baker lived at Mom Charleston's, a theatrical boardinghouse on Broad Street after marrying her second husband, William Baker. Philadelphia's Ernest "Chubby" Checker created the Twist, which launched a craze that swept dance halls at home and abroad. Dance teacher Marian Cuyjet's star student, Judith Jamison, gained acclaim in the dance world with grandeur, power, and grace. Philadanco, founded in 1970 by Philadelphian Joan Myers Brown, hosted the International Conference on Black Dance Companies, attracting more than 140 dance companies in 1988 and 1989.

The Arthur Hall Dancer. In dance circles, choreographer and dancer Arthur Hall was an established name during the 1960s and 1970s in Philadelphia and elsewhere. Hall founded the Ile Ife Black Humanitarian Center in Philadelphia, which was the home of Arthur Hall's Dance Ensemble. Shown is Gail Thomas performing a difficult pose.

STOP THE PUSHER. This broadside illustrates that the drug traffic was a major threat to the entire city of Philadelphia. In the late 1970s, an effort was begun to stop the drug menace, as shown in this poster issued in 1976 by the Philadelphia Anti-Poverty Action Committee.

ODUNDE. Founded in Philadelphia by Lois A. Fernandez in April 1975, Odunde is an annual African American festival held in South Philadelphia on Twenty-third and South Streets. The word *odunde,* meaning "Happy New Year," originated with the Yoruba people of Nigeria. Since the first festival, Odunde has grown in scope and magnitude. Each succeeding year has brought increasing involvement from interested persons across the country. In June 2000, Odunde celebrated its 25th anniversary.

THE FIRE ON OSAGE AVENUE. On May 13, 1985, a bomb containing as much as 3.5 pounds of high-grade explosives was dropped from a state police helicopter onto a roof of row houses in a residential African American neighborhood on Osage Avenue. The resulting fire killed 11 members of MOVE, a radical back-to-nature group. Fifty-three houses were destroyed and 262 middle-class African Americans were left homeless. Charles Bowser, a prominent African American attorney, wrote in his book *Let the Bunker Burn*, "As unreasonable as it was, it happened . . . . This book is written because it happened and it must not be forgotten.

ROBERT N.C. NIX SR. AND JR. Pictured in this photograph is one of America's great father and son political teams. Robert N.C. Nix Sr. was elected to Congress in 1958 and was the first African American congressman from the Commonwealth of Pennsylvania. His son, Robert N.C. Nix Jr. became a Pennsylvania state Supreme Court justice.

THE MILLION WOMAN MARCH. In October 1997, nearly 1 million women and others from various parts of the world assembled in Philadelphia on the Benjamin Franklin Parkway. The Million Woman March was organized by two Philadelphia African American women, Phile Chionesu and Asia Coney. A group of women is shown walking the area of the Philadelphia Museum of Art, where the day-long main event took place.

THE MAYOR JOHN F. STREET CAMPAIGN POSTER. In 2000, Philadelphians elected their second African American mayor, John F. Street. Mayor Street, a Temple University Law School graduate, had previously served on the Philadelphia City Council for the Fifth Council District and was city council president for a total of 19 years before his election as mayor.

ACKNOWLEDGMENTS

I owe an enormous debt of gratitude to John W. Mosley, who dedicated more than 30 years capturing the images of people and events pertaining to Philadelphia's African American community. I would like to thank Lisa K. Fitch for her contribution and help typing the manuscript. This book is offered for scholars, students, visitors, and the public as a record of a historic city and its African American community. This book is not intended to be a comprehensive study of African American life in Philadelphia. I take full responsibility for unintended omissions or factual errors.

Suggested Reading:

Ballard, Allen B. *One More Day's Journey.* New York: McGraw Hill, 1984.

Brown, Ira V. *The Negro in Pennsylvania History.* The Pennsylvania History Studies, 1970.

Dubin, Murray. *South Philadelphia, Mummers, Memories and the Melrose Diner.* Philadelphia: Temple University Press, 1996.

Dubois, W.E.B. *The Philadelphia Negro: A Social Study*. Boston: Ginn and Co., 1899.

Lane, Roger. *William Dorsey's Philadelphia and Ours.* New York: Oxford University Press, 1991.

Nash, Gary. *Forging Freedom: The Formation of Philadelphia's Black Community 1720–1840.* Cambridge, Mass. 1988.

Other books by Charles L. Blockson:

Pennsylvania's Black History
Black Genealogy
The Underground Railroad in Pennsylvania
The Underground Railroad: First-Person Narratives of Escapes to Freedom in the North, 1987
A Commented Bibliography of One Hundred and One Influential Books by and about People of African Descent (1556–1982)
Catalogue of the Charles L. Blockson Afro American Collection
The Journey of John W. Mosley
African Americans in Pennsylvania: A History and Guide
Hippocrene Guide to the Underground Railroad
Damn Rare